A TERRIFYING NOVEL
OF SEXUAL REVENGE

Kathy Jacquard, recently separated from her husband, hoped that her job as night nurse at the
Roget Special Clinic would take her mind off Ed.
Confident that she could bring her special patient
out of a three-year coma, she tried the only way
she could think of to arouse Patrick—and realized too late that a comatose madman had fallen
in love with her.

But was it just a madman lying in Room 15? Or
was it something much, much worse. . . .

PATRICK

IT WILL SHOCK YOU.

PATRICK

KEITH
HETHERINGTON

AVON
PUBLISHERS OF BARD, CAMELOT AND DISCUS BOOKS

AVON BOOKS
A division of
The Hearst Corporation
959 Eighth Avenue
New York, New York 10019

First Avon Printing, January, 1980

AVON TRADEMARK REG. U.S. PAT. OFF. AND IN
OTHER COUNTRIES, MARCA REGISTRADA,
HECHO EN U.S.A.

Printed in the U.S.A.

PATRICK

Prologue

Patrick had decided to kill his mother. There was no other way. She had to die.

The decision had come to him with surprising ease, within minutes of his arrival at the dark and empty house in Collingwood. He had stripped half-naked in his room, turned on the electric radiator and laid down on the bed, curled up in the foetal position, briefly returning to the warmth and silence and security of the womb. A retreat.

His own bed always had that effect on him—and he had slept in everything from a humidicrib, after he had entered this life two months prematurely, through bassinettes, cots, bunks, camp stretchers, to sleeping-bags, normal beds and, once, a waterbed. Countless times in his life his bed had been the only refuge.

No one believed that he actually remembered the time he had spent in that humidicrib, monitored by tubes and wires and tiny electrodes taped to his barely-living body. They said it was post-association of images gleaned from pictures and films seen in later life of premature babies struggling for survival under plastic, tended day and night by nurses and doctors. They said he could not possibly remember that time.

He let them smile smugly in the assurance of their convictions. But Patrick *knew*. He remembered every detail—the fight for each tiny breath in an effort to expand minute lungs and oxygenate thin blood; the jarring of his frail frame with each concussion of the pulsing heart not much bigger than a fifty-cent piece;

7

the traumatic terror and pain of full-sized needles violating his paper-thin skin; seeing the world as a succession of peering, expressionless faces, eyes above sterile masks, gloved fingers prodding, probing . . .

He had not gained those memories from films. He had *lived* the experience.

Just as he had lived that other experience ten years later, the one that had never left him, the one that had ruined his life. The one that made him decide to kill his mother.

Something had happened to her money, the monthly cheques she lived on suddenly stopped coming. He never knew the details, only that he saw her grow old in a week while she lived in hope that there had merely been some delay in the mail. Then, after the realization that there would be no more cheques, she had taken to crying a lot and drinking more. They moved from the old house in Kew to a small flat in Prahran and finally to an Abbotsford bed-sitter, where he had to sleep on a camp stretcher beside his mother's huge brass bed.

He knew she always had a lot of men visiting her, even vaguely understood what happened when they went into her bedroom. But, in a room of his own, lost in his imaginings, emulating Robinson Crusoe or the father who he had never known, the father who had deserted his mother even before he was born, it had not concerned Patrick.

In the bed-sitter it was different. He couldn't help but hear—and see—what went on in the big double bed. It hadn't bothered him unduly. Normally it meant only about twenty minutes of giggling, fumbling and mild thrashing about, after which he could go back to sleep.

Until the Night of The Pig.

Thud-thud-thud-thud. The wall beside his ear had echoed hollowly, and Patrick clawed his way up from the depths of sleep through terrifying visions of ghouls or monster rats gnawing their way through the fungus-scabbed walls in their efforts to get at him. His eyes flew open, his heart hammered and his belly quivered

8

as he stared uncomprehendingly at the dark figures writhing on the bed above him.

The man was like an animal, grunting, pig-like, driving a cry from his mother that was part pain, part pleasure. Then the man's scrabbling foot skidded off the edge of the bedframe and smashed into Patrick's face. Blood squirted from his nostrils. Patrick cried out but the sound was lost in the violence of the bed as the brass knob on one of the corner posts rapped against the wall with such force that it jarred loose flakes of calcified paint and plaster.

Terrified, teeth biting down on the threadbare blankets as they grew wetter with the blood oozing from his nose, Patrick listened to the man's rasping and the bedpost's ever increasing tattoo: *thud-thud-thud-thud*. He began to cry in great choking sobs as his mother started to scream softly, gasping as if she was suffocating, beating and tearing at the man's humping back, pleading, cursing, hysterical. Patrick tried to swallow the sickness that rose in his throat, utterly terrified, afraid that the man was killing her, afraid that he too would be killed.

Suddenly it ended and his mother must have heard one of Patrick's half-stifled sobs. She tried to get up to see if he was all right but the man—The Pig, as he thought of him now—wouldn't let her. They wrestled briefly and then the terrifying violence started all over again. This time Patrick had been unable to restrain himself. He had vomited.

Next morning, his mother, bruised and spent, stood by while the man thrashed him and made him clean up the mess.

There were other bed-sitters, other lovers, but none like The Pig. Eventually, they moved into a house at Collingwood, but by that time the pattern had been set and the sexual side of Patrick's life had been ruined.

Only a thin wall separated his bedroom from his mother's and sometimes he awoke in the night to hear her gasps and moans as she approached climax. Patrick's gorge would rise, and he would race for the toilet.

It carried right through into his adult life to the time when he was old enough to want to bed a woman of his own. Everything went well, considering it was the first time for both of them, until she began to whimper at the approach of climax. Her cries and movements immediately plunged Patrick back through time to the Night of The Pig. Abruptly, the moaning body beneath him was his mother's. Worse, he saw himself as The Pig.

He wilted instantly.

It was a long time before he plucked up enough courage to try to make love to another woman. It too ended in disaster, a dismal failure. As was the third time. And the fourth. The seductions were free of problems until the moment the girl began to moan. Then— a brief hiatus and humiliation.

Perseverance gained him nothing except indignity and contempt. Especially after that slut spread it around the university campus. He found her and hit her, and she spat in his face. He had fled in shame, run to this darkened room where he now lay on the bed, still curled in the foetal position, and it was here the words of Oscar Wilde had flowed through his mind, "Yet each man kills the thing he loves . . ." Yes, it was here, malevolent and alone, he decided to kill his mother, decided that he *had* to kill her.

Now he merely waited for her to return with her latest lover.

It was long after midnight when he heard the car stop outside, the tipsy laughter, the clinking bottles and the stumbling up the stairs. He sat up and leant against the wall.

"Hey! Wha' about that lunatic son of yours?" slurred the man. He sounded young, like all of his mother's lovers. The last one had been even younger than Patrick himself.

"Patrick's away for the weekend," his mother replied, her voice telling him she was once again stupid with booze. "And he's not loony."

"Coulda fooled me."

"He's very brainy. Prac . . . pract . . . nearly a Bachelor of Science."

10

"Bachelor of Bullshit!"

Then she gave a sudden squeal. "Naughty! Can't you wait?" she giggled.

"Since you ask—no!"

The stupid words and meaningless laughter left Patrick unmoved. Perhaps his breathing quickened slightly. He concentrated on his plan, knowing his mother's routine after the love-making was over. She always . . . He went suddenly rigid. His teeth clenched, his eyes snapped open and stared almost maniacally . . .

Thud-thud-thud-thud! The corner post of his mother's bed began hammering the wall behind his head, barely inches away. Rhythmically, interminably.

He had no idea how much time had passed before he became aware of the sound of running water. Slowly the room came back into focus. He felt the light touch of heat from the radiator. It was still dark.

"Wha', wha're you doin' now, love?" The man's voice was muffled.

"Taking a bath," his mother called from down the hall. With a touch of coquetry she added, "Want to join me?"

"I'll be in that!" The sound of bare feet padded down the hall, stumbling a little. "An' I mean *join* you!"

"God! Aren't you ever satisfied?" But she sounded pleased, anticipating.

Patrick waited, listening to them sliding into the water, splashing about. His mother *"whoopsed!"* and he heard a great gout of water spill over the edge of the bath onto the tiled floor. His mother laughed. The man let out a surprised yell, tinged with pleasure.

Patrick rolled off the bed and groped about the floor until he found a pair of runners. He pulled them on, not bothering to tie the laces. Then he padded across to a cupboard, took out a long extension lead and went back to where the radiator glowed on the floor. Patrick switched it off and, before the blood colour had faded from the element, unplugged the heater, connected the extension lead, and pushed the plug back into the wall socket. He switched the power back on and watched

11

the element glow brilliantly, feeling the scorching heat against his skin.

He picked up the radiator in his right hand, the coiled lead in his left. He fancied he could feel the minute pulsing of the electricity as it surged into the element.

Moving silently down the dark hall, he dropped the coils of the extension lead carefully, approaching the bathroom and the wet sounds and giggles of the lovers. The door was not quite closed and he could see them through the gap.

Just as Patrick opened the door, the man's face appeared over his mother's left shoulder. His eyes were closed. Slowly, his eyes opened and he saw Patrick. His stare widened and he tried to squirm out from under the woman, making inarticulate sounds in the back of his throat.

Patrick's eyes were icy, his face set. With a deliberate, jerky movement, he hurled the radiator at the bath.

The man raised an arm in an attempt to keep it from striking the woman. It glanced off her head and the stench of burning hair instantly filled the steamy room. She cried out, startled, floundered around, spilling gallons of water over the side. The man's eyes were like ping-pong balls as he strived desperately to prevent the heater from touching the water. He made a grab for it but slipped and his groping hands jammed it against the woman's wet back. She screamed. The man hysterically pawed at it. Skin and tissue ripped away, leaving the imprint of the hot metal grid on her back.

The man managed to cry out as the scarlet element tumbled into the water, "Christ, Patrick . . . your own mother!"

The heater struck the water in a blinding flash, followed by a strange, zipping, sizzling sound. The lights went out in a shower of sparks but Patrick could see their bodies convulsing as they died. The cord yanked tight, slackened, forming a series of irregular loops on the flooded tiles.

His face a cold mask, Patrick stepped forward to examine his handiwork. He tripped on the loose lace

12

of his runners. His other foot caught in one of the loops in the extension lead and he stumbled. The cord came free of the heater plug and the live socket fell into the spilled bathwater. Patrick's hands went out before him instinctively as he fell. He had time for a single gasp as the cold, wet tiles touched his naked flesh. Then the water entered the still-charged socket and there was another flash of sparks.

Patrick's body seemed to erupt, snapping rigid, as it was catapulted half-way across the room. His head smashed into the washbasin stand, cracking his skull.

As he lay there, confused brain cells were annihilated one by one, arteries, engorged with blood, erupted into torn tissues and nerve fibres withered. His heart and lungs virtually ceased to function. He was transported to the very edge of Death.

But somewhere in the depths of his brain something stirred feebly, struggling for survival.

The remnant of a mysterious force that, for want of a better term, was called "Life."

Chapter One

Tap-drag-tap-drag-tap-drag. The four-pronged walking
stick had two of the shock-absorbing rubbers missing
and the uncovered struts scraped along the highly-
polished linoleum of the clinic hallway. A bent figure,
almost entirely enshrouded in a voluminous Army
greatcoat, thrust out the walking aid with a thin, shaky
arm, planted the four feet firmly before trusting it to
take his weight as he moved pyjama-clad legs forward
in another step towards the side doors.

On his head was a moth-eaten and misshapen slouch
hat of World War I vintage, with the original puggaree
still around the crown. A light- and dark-blue colour
patch was hanging from the side of the puggaree's
windings, precariously supported by only two retaining
stitches. Beneath the hat a thin, silver-stubbled face
stared out, the skin leathery with old age, the rheumy,
once-clear blue eyes tight in concentration as the walking aid jerked and dragged forward again, and the thin
legs carried his frail body closer to the door.

The cuffs of the pyjamas flapped, stained yellow with
dried urine. He reached his goal and the walking aid
took his weight shakily as he grabbed the highly-
polished brass handle, turned it and eased the door
open. The distant rumble of evening peak-hour traffic
assailed him. It was a pleasant hour, apart from the
traffic sounds. The sky was pastel-coloured, a child
laughed somewhere down the block and high up a flight
of birds winged their way homeward. The old man
stepped out onto the tiled porch, turned sharp left, and

15

presented himself before a cupboard-like box. He opened the box, looked in at the meters with their spinning silver discs and crawling dial needles, and selected a switch. The gnarled hand grasped the handle and paused briefly, as if savouring the feel of the cool, smooth metal, and then with a look of determination he pulled the lever firmly downwards.

Instantly, from above his head came the sizzle, hum and whine of electricity, the *click-click* of tiny relays and switches, the arcing of neon gas surging through bent glass tubing and a red sign lit up, uncertainly, but burning out its message: EMERGENCY ENTRANCE. The "E" and "N" of ENTRANCE flickered on and off, the sizzling and clicking continued interminably.

The old man looked up at the sign with a satisfaction far deeper than one would have thought for such a simple accomplishment. But it had been his job for the past—what?—must be almost twenty years now, and when your guts were half blown away and the bottoms of both lungs were rotten and foul with the remnants of mustard gas, and muscles were flabby, atrophied, barely co-ordinating, the nightly duty of switching on the clinic sign was something to feel proud about.

He was about to turn back into the huge building, a sprawling, double-storied old mansion, when he saw the girl coming down the path. She was a pretty thing, mid-twenties he reckoned, blonde, pert, with a thin waist. She was carrying a manila folder, but instead of going inside the girl stopped at the foot of the porch steps and smiled up at him. Her teeth were white and even, her face pleasant, and there was a warmth in her eyes that he had seen long ago, in the mud and filth of the trenches at Passchendaele as the Red Cross nurses moved among the maimed and wounded.

"Excuse me, sir . . ."

He loved her for that "sir!"

". . . Is this the Roget Special Clinic?" Her voice was smooth and modulated. She blinked in surprise as the old man shuffled his feet and raised a scrawny arm and

16

she realized he was trying to stand to attention and give her a salute!

"Cap'n Albert Fraser at your service, Miss." Then, conspiratorily, he leaned towards her, the thin arm that rested on the walking aid trembled with strain. "Beware the Hun. He's mobilizin' for a push."

The girl's smile tightened a little at the edges, but then widened again. "Thank you for the warning, Captain. Er . . . *Is* this the Roget Special Clinic?"

He winked ponderously. She waited for him to say something else but all he did was smile, showing his gums with a few rotted stumps of teeth.

"Perhaps I had better ask inside. I'm Kathy Jacquard. I have an appointment with Matron Cassidy. I hope to work here."

"Cassidy?" echoed the Captain. "Fine orficer. Second dugout down the line. Bit 'ard on the men, but discipline's what's needed if we're gonna stand against the Hun." Then, with an abrupt switch that left Kathy a little stunned, he jerked a thumb to the sizzling electric sign and said, in an entirely different voice, an *old* voice, "Just switched the sign on. Been me job for twenty years. Never missed a night. Nor will I. The first time that sign don't go on at dusk, you can call the undertaker, 'cause it'll mean I'm dead . . ." He cackled, then suddenly sobered. "Who're you, Miss?"

Kathy came up the steps, smiled and patted his hand. "Kathy Jacquard, Captain. Thank you for your information. Can I help you back inside?"

He drew his hand away sharply. "Can manage meself," he growled and watched as she shrugged and went past him into the big hall. Then his stump-studded gums bared and he chuckled softly to himself as he followed her into the hall, his walking stick tap-dragging with him.

Kathy swiftly lost any confidence she might have felt while talking with Captain Fraser when she faced Matron Cassidy in her high-ceilinged office. The Matron was stern-faced though her features were basically pleasant enough. Her manner was abrupt, a "full-of-business" kind of brusqueness that could well have

17

been a mark for her own uncertainty when facing strangers—even those after such junior positions as night nurse.

Matron Cassidy had metal-framed spectacles dangling around her neck on a glittering gold chain and she lifted these, adjusted them, and read the papers she had taken from Kathy's manila folder. She peered over the tops of the glasses once and Kathy, sitting stiffly in the metal chair across the enormous desk from the Matron, felt an inexplicable knotting of her belly. Then the Matron returned to her reading, flipped swiftly through the papers and let them drop onto the desk, placing her hands flat on top of them. She nudged the glasses from her nose and allowed them to fall to her chest on the chain.

Matron stared at Kathy across the wide expanse of desk, then abruptly lifted one hand, stabbed at a button on the intercom beside her, leaning slightly towards it but continuing to look at the girl.

"Roget," crackled a voice metallically out of the intercom.

"I have the applicant with me, Doctor," Matron said.

Kathy was not sure if she heard him hiss out a mild curse or not, but he sounded pleasant enough when he spoke again. "All right. I'll be in."

Matron Cassidy released the button, sat up straight, at last looking away from Kathy and picking up the papers from the folder again. Kathy stirred nervously, she knew what Matron was going to say.

"Your last reference is dated three years ago, Mrs. Jacquard. You haven't worked as a nursing sister since then?"

Kathy shook her head. "I stopped when I got married."

Matron frowned slightly. "English, aren't you?"

Kathy nodded.

"Haven't worked at nursing in this country at all?"

"No."

"Hmmm." Matron sounded mildly disapproving. "Three years is a long time to be out of this profession, Mrs. Jacquard. So many new techniques to master, new

18

drugs to learn about . . . Not to mention a different disciplinary structure."

"I'm sure I could manage that, Matron."

The Matron merely looked at her for what seemed like an interminable time and then abruptly asked, "Could you handle some typing from time to time?"

Kathy, a little surprised but now hopeful for the first time since entering the office, nodded swiftly. "Oh, yes."

"Children?"

"Pardon? I mean, yes, I have worked with children. I think one of my references mentions . . ."

"I meant have you any children of your own?" Matron snapped.

"Uh . . . no," Kathy answered a little lamely.

"What about *Mister* Jacquard? He doesn't mind you doing shift work?"

"Well, we're . . . separated."

"I see." There was a distinct coolness about Matron Cassidy now. She made a brief note. "Why?"

Kathy frowned, cocking her head slightly, not at all sure that she had the right to ask that, debating whether or not to answer and wondering if it would affect her chances of getting the job. However, Matron glanced up and said, "Of course, it's really none of my business, but let's be frank, Mrs. Jacquard, we at the clinic are not interested in restless housewives merely looking for something to fill in their spare time and who will resign at the first threat of a soiled bedpan."

"Oh no, Matron, I mean . . ."

The Matron ignored her. "Why did you choose the Roget Clinic?"

"Well, the Agency said . . ."

Once again Matron ignored Kathy's attempted explanation. "Because we are only a small clinic, some applicants presume that our standards are, shall we say, less rigid."

"Well no, I . . ."

"And, because of this misconception, we tend to attract certain—types."

"Types?"

"Types, Mrs. Jacquard."

"I don't think I follow you . . ."

Matron rattled off a list of "types" with the staccato sureness of a machine gun. "Lesbians, nymphomaniacs, enema specialists, algolagniacs, necrophiliacs, pedophiliacs, exhibitionists, voyeurs . . . *Now* do you follow me?"

Kathy felt her cheeks burning, more at Matron's treatment of her than the terms she had used. "Yes, I understand."

"Really? Disease, like God, Mrs. Jacquard, works in mysterious ways. It can don the mask of perversion and spread like a cancer through a hospital staff. We had a classic in here only last week, seated in that chair where you are now, applying for work as an orderly." Matron leaned forward a little, eyes squinting slightly in her intensity. She looked every one of her forty-three years as her mouth twisted when she announced, "*His* little quirk, as it turned out, was to sneak down to the laundry at night and paint himself with excreta." She sat back abruptly, toying with the glasses on the chain. "Shocked, Mrs. Jacquard?"

"No," Kathy lied, hoping her face was blank.

"Well, you should be. It shocked me. And I have been a witness to just about any kind of vileness you can name during my years in this profession."

After a short pause, Kathy licked her lips and tried a brief smile. "I, I can assure you that . . ."

She broke off as the door opened. A cadaverous man in his fifties with a skull-shaped face, protruding forehead and eyes that seemed to see things that other people didn't, stood there looking towards Matron Cassidy, thin eyebrows raised quizzically.

"Oh, come in Doctor. Mrs. Jacquard—Doctor Roget."

"I'm pleased to meet you, Doctor," Kathy said.

Roget's mouth moved in a quick, flickering smile and he thrust bony hands into the pockets of his sloppy, spotted dust-coat. Then he turned his attention to the Matron.

"Have my frogs arrived yet?"

20

"Not yet, Doctor."

Kathy again heard that faint hissing, smothered curse that had come through the intercom earlier. The expression on his face didn't change. He seemed very intent about something, yet at the same time almost vague about his surroundings.

"Chase it up, will you?"

"I'll make a note," Matron said, doing precisely that. Then, lifting Kathy's manila folder and offering it to Roget she said, "Mrs. Jacquard's qualifications are adequate, though she hasn't worked in Australia as . . ."

Roget ignored the proffered folder, flicked his rather bulbous eyes to Kathy and she swore that they changed focus, like a slide projector automatically adjusting the picture on the screen. "Had experience with unconscious patients?"

"Yes, Doctor."

"Cerebral monitoring, EEG's, Fourier Analysis, dialysis procedures?"

"A little. I used to . . ."

Matron's voice cut across Kathy's reply, coldly, flatly, as she again offered Roget the folder containing Kathy's papers. "She comes to us in the wake of an unstable domestic situation, Doctor."

Roget's eyes skirmished with Matron's in a brief visual exchange that had Kathy involuntarily biting her lower lip. There was a short silence in the office. Kathy was aware of a vague buzzing sound, frowned, looked up. The fluorescent tube above Matron's desk was flickering slightly, gases writhing inside the glass, swirling like the tense apprehension inside Kathy at this moment.

"Hire her," Roget said firmly and, as Kathy brought her gaze swiftly down on him, he shot her that snake-like smile as he turned and went out, leaving a kind of momentary vacuum behind him. Matron let the folder fall onto her polished desk, her face expressionless as she stared at the door that Roget closed very firmly as he went out. Then, without looking at Kathy, she stabbed at a call button on her desk, picked up the folder, and thrust it across the desk towards Kathy.

"I . . . have the job?"

As if in one final attempt to discourage her, Matron sighed resignedly and told her, "Doctor Roget owns this hospital. It gives him the privilege of having the final say in borderline cases such as yours." She stood up, taller than Kathy by a few inches, looking down at the younger woman. "But let me make it very clear indeed to you, Mrs. Jacquard, I am the boss cocky here. I set high standards and they have to. be met. I will not tolerate slackness or slovenly work of any kind." In an almost casual voice she added, "The salary is minimal, the hours abominable, and I will insist on the right to terminate your employment without notice." She gave Kathy a faint, crooked smile. "If you can accept those conditions—and others that I will impose, I warn you!—then yes, Mrs. Jacquard, you have the job!"

"That's . . . fine. Thank you, Matron." Kathy couldn't keep the relief out of her voice and Matron Cassidy looked at her sharply.

"When can you begin?"

"Why . . . tonight . . . Immediately, I guess."

"We don't *guess* here, Mrs. Jacquard."

"Right away, then."

Matron nodded as the door opened and a tall, well-proportioned girl about Kathy's age, wearing the nursing uniform of the Roget Clinic, looked expectantly towards Matron Cassidy. Kathy thought she was beautiful with her dark hair and dark eyes. She was sensual, but naturally so. With her figure, she would never have to work at it.

"You buzzed, Matron?"

"Yes. This is Sister Jacquard—Sister Williams. She is going to start as a night nurse. I want you to get her a uniform and then have her relieve Sister Panicale."

Kathy was not sure if she imagined that Williams stiffened, but she was certain the smile she had given Kathy suddenly froze around the edges. Her voice sounded strained.

"Sister Panicale, Matron?"

"Yes," Matron was impatient with her, "in Room 15."

22

"I see," Williams said and her smile had gone altogether as she stood aside, holding the door as she spoke to Kathy. "This way, Sister," she said tautly.

Kathy felt a bit wooden as she moved towards the door, wondering what was so special about Room 15.

"I wasn't even sure I was in the right place when I saw that old man in the Army coat appear on the porch," Kathy chatted to Paula Williams as they walked towards the lift. Kathy was now trim and smart in a crisp blue uniform. She laughed a little. "I thought I must have come to a Salvation Army Home by mistake."

Paula Williams smiled, pushing the lift button. "Old Captain Fraser could give you that impression, I guess. Harmless old sod. Wets himself a lot. Think he's still fighting World War I." Her thumb stabbed the button again several times, without result. "Damn. We'd better take the stairs. Lift's playing up again."

As they climbed the ornate stairway to the upper floors, Williams said, "This is the craziest place for electrical troubles. Really weird things happen at times. Lights flickering, going out at the wrong times, coming *on* at the wrong times!" She turned and smiled. "And the number of times that darn lift has jammed between floors. One of these days everything will just go *phut!* and we'll lose all our patients on life-support."

Kathy frowned. "Surely there's an emergency generator?"

"Oh, sure. Works, too, but the way things happen here, I'd never be surprised if it gives up the ghost just when it's needed most." She led the way down a brightly lit corridor and, near the end, pointed to Room 17. "That's your Captain Fraser's dugout, as he calls it. He'll be your neighbour."

Kathy looked at her puzzledly and Paula stopped before the next door with the numerals "15" painted on it in dark green. "While you're on duty here, I mean." She opened the door and gestured to Kathy to enter. "Come and meet our star patient."

Kathy went in swiftly, briefly looking at the form of the patient lying prostrate on a bed that was sur-

23

rounded by an almost overwhelming mass of life-support machinery. She noticed that a dialysis unit was connected, dark red blood flowing through the transparent exchange tubes. Then Williams said, "This is Sister Panicale—Sister Jacquard."

Kathy smiled at the dark-skinned little nurse sitting in a corner knitting. A box of tissues and a paperbag stuffed with used ones were beside her. She smiled nervously and reached for a fresh tissue, blew her red-tipped nose violently.

"Soddy, goh a bud col," she sniffed, scrubbing at her nostrils and increasing the redness.

"You should be in bed," Kathy said sympathetically.

"Carn," Panicale said and gestured towards the bed. "He's godda be looked after."

Kathy turned to look at the patient properly for the first time as Williams explained to Panicale that Kathy would be taking over this noon-to-nine shift and that the dark girl could now resume her normal duties on Ward One. Before Kathy even had time to notice that the patient was a young man, Panicale had gathered all her gear up into her arms and started hurriedly for the door, trailing a ball of yarn, eager to go.

"You'll have to monitor the dialysis," Panicale said to Kathy as she hurried by, winding in her yarn. "Anudder two hours. Goo' luh."

Kathy frowned slightly but Williams was doing her best to smother a laugh.

"Don't worry about Panicale. She's frightened of her own shadow, has diarrhoea every time night shift comes around. I don't know why she bothers. I think she dies a little every time she has to do duty here."

"Why?" Kathy turned to the bed and studied the patient now. He was a youngish man, mid-twenties perhaps, handsome, his chest barely moving. He was rigged up to drip bottles suspended from a stainless steel stand and the breeze through the open window rattled them gently. Kathy looked at the position of his feet under the sheet and could see that he was tall.

He lay unmoving, large blue eyes staring straight up at the ceiling.

24

Paula Williams moved across and closed the casement window. Outside the EMERGENCY sign fizzled and glowed. "I'm not sure whether Panicale is trying to give herself pneumonia or him." She nodded in the patient's direction and after locking the window came and stood beside Kathy looking down at the bed. "Our star boarder. Patrick. Comatose, of course. You will be specialling him, responsible for monitoring the life-support and so on."

"Why aren't his eyes sutured shut?" Kathy asked.

Williams shrugged. Not sounding terribly interested, she responded, "Roget's orders. You'll be expected to keep his eyes bathed and lubricated."

Kathy looked around at the mass of machinery, automatically checking the dialysis blood-exchange dials as she noted the oxygen bottles, respirator, oscilloscope monitoring screens, a defibrillator with the rubber shock pads at the ends of their wires, the head-harness and electrodes and graph rolls and an electroencephalograph apparatus. "My God, we're certainly doing our best to keep him alive. There must be a fortune in here!"

"Roget's orders once again."

Kathy stepped closer to the head of the bed and looked down into the sightless eyes. "Hello Patrick," she said softly. "I'll take care of you all right."

"Don't waste your breath, Sister. He's dead."

Kathy spun abruptly, looking startled. Paula smiled slightly, pleased that she had shocked the other girl.

"Oh technically he's alive, I guess, insomuch as he pumps blood—with a little help from the dialysis unit every so often—and he breaths thanks to the respirator, and he lives on glucose drips and urinates and defaecates, but that is where it ends. I doubt that you will get much conversation out of him. He doesn't even blink. He's been in a coma for three years.

Kathy tensed. "Three *years!*" she whispered. "What happened? Car accident?" Her face was warm with compassion as she looked down at the motionless man in the bed.

"Accident of some sort. Don't know the whole story, but I do know he was originally in Lochart."

Kathy was puzzled. "But that's . . ."

Paula nodded, interrupting. "Yeah, institution for the criminally insane. Like I said, I don't know the details. Doctor Roget says his brain is just dead meat."

"What a waste," Kathy said sympathetically.

"Waste of space if you ask me. All our new sisters start off with Patrick." She sighed. "Anyway, sister, such as he is, he's all yours."

Kathy frowned, shaking her head slowly. "A special nurse for a patient like this—it's a bit extravagant for a hospital this size, isn't it? I mean, who pays for it all?" She swept an arm around, indicating the machines, then stepped swiftly to the dialysis unit to adjust a knob. The flow-rate needle dropped slightly and Williams nodded in approval.

"You're on the ball, I'll say that for you. I guess the Government pays, I don't know. Whoever foots the bill, it's a waste of money, I reckon."

"No chance of him improving at all?"

Williams shrugged. "Been too long in a coma. Roget says even if he did regain consciousness he'd only have the intelligence of a penicillin culture."

Kathy looked up from making another adjustment at the machine, glanced down at Patrick. Her look said "too bad," though she didn't speak. Williams glanced at her watch.

"Look, Matron will be in her office until 6:30. Doctor Roget works till all hours. Otherwise the desk nurse will sign you out at nine. You be okay now?"

Kathy nodded, smiling, moving to the head of the bed and leaning over Patrick to tuck the sheet snugly around his shoulders. She stared down into his statue-like face.

"We will be fine, won't we Patrick?" She turned her head towards the other girl, feeling that she should try to be off-hand too. "Not much danger of him chasing me down the corridors."

Williams' face remained deadpan. "I'd say it's unlikely."

Kathy flushed at the failure of her words to amuse.

26

Embarrassed, she said, "I'm sorry. That was in pretty bad taste."

"Not really. You have to joke about it when you're stuck in here with a living corpse for hours on end."

Kathy smiled faintly at Williams' reassurance and bent down again, fussing with the sheet. "Well, I think Patrick and I are going to get along just . . ."

She gasped and jumped back as Patrick spat in her face.

Chapter Two

Shocked, Kathy automatically took the towel that Paula Williams handed her and mopped at her wet face.

"That's another thing," Paula said off-handedly. "He spits. Doctor Roget says it is some sort of motor-nerve reflex. But he's only guessing. No one really knows why he does it."

Kathy frowned, still mopping her face though it was dry by now. "He seemed to do it . . . on purpose!"

Williams laughed. "Patrick? He doesn't even crap on purpose! It happens, but he has no control over it."

Kathy didn't look quite convinced. "It was almost as if he'd heard us making fun of him."

Paula laughed again. "Sweetie, you'll wind up being an inmate here too if you start thinking like that! He can't hear, he can't see, he can't feel, he just . . . *can't!* Don't worry about it."

"But how can you be sure about those things?" Kathy insisted quietly.

"Doctor Roget says so and when Doctor Roget speaks, we listen. Besides, he's continually experimenting with Patrick, knows his condition better than anyone else."

"Experimenting with him? Like a guinea pig?"

Williams sighed. "You *have* been away from the profession for a long time. Too long by the sounds of it. I'll leave you to it. And better be careful what you think." She laughed and winked at Kathy's puzzled face. "Just in case Patrick reads your mind."

She went out, closing the door and Kathy concentrated on the unit, then, satisfied, walked across to the main life-support apparatus, looking at the dials and monitoring screens. Patrick's heartbeat barely registered as the electronic scan crossed the glass screen, but the beat seemed regular enough. The pulse rate was very low, about the mid-fifties. Respiration, barely adequate. Brain activity—nil.

Patrick was almost in a state of hibernation. Or suspended animation. They were almost the same thing, except that . . .

She stopped thinking about it abruptly. She didn't know why, she just felt uneasy. She moved over to Patrick, placed a hand gently on his cheek. The flesh was cool, wax-like. She held the back of her hand just in front of his nostrils, and could barely feel his exhalations. Suddenly she jumped as the drip bottles clinked together and paper scrapped and flapped. She saw the pages of Patrick's medical chart on the clipboard hanging over the end of the bed, rustling in a breeze.

Frowning, Kathy glanced across the room. That was strange, she thought. The window was open again.

The tram rattled to a stop in the dark Carlton street and Kathy Jacquard stepped down wearily. She hurried to the footpath and walked on at a steady clip, turning down a side street and heading towards a small Italian delicatessen and pizza bar.

One of the cars that had been in the line behind the tram, a battered blue Holden a couple of years old, turned down the side street and pulled into the kerb. The lights were switched off but the motor idled softly. A cigarette glowed through the windscreen.

Kathy came out of the delicatessen carrying a large paper bag and pizza carton. She seemed to have trouble managing the load as well as her shoulderbag, the strap of which kept slipping. It was when she turned her head slightly to adjust the strap that she noticed the car back up the street, crawling along very slowly with just parking lights on. For a moment she stopped, frowning, annoyed at the chill that went through her. She distributed her load more evenly, turned and hurried down the street towards her block of flats.

29

Just before she went through the main door she looked back. The blue Holden was at the corner, pulled into the kerb now, parking lights still on. Her teeth tugged lightly at her lower lip as she went inside and up to her own flat on the second floor. She was getting jumpy she thought as she took out the groceries and opened the pizza carton top to allow it to cool. It must be working at night again—and in that creepy clinic with . . . what had Williams called Patrick? . . . yes, a living corpse.

It was sort of uncanny sitting in that sterile room, the only sounds the muted *pock-pock* of the life-support system, or the tiny *clink* of the drip-feed bottles swinging on their stainless steel gallows in the breeze from the window. She still didn't know how it had opened again. She was sure Paula Williams had locked it . . .

Kathy sighed determinedly and put away the groceries, brewed some Nescafé, and drank it with a couple of slices of the pizza. She looked around at the sparsely-stocked cupboards and across the counter into the lounge room with her partly unpacked tea-chests. She had plenty to think about here without dwelling too much on the Roget Clinic and its inmates.

There were all her things to unpack and find places for, she wanted to re-paper the feature wall of the lounge and probably paint the other walls and ceiling.

Washing up at the sink, she moved the curtains aside on an impulse and looked down into the street. The blue Holden was right outside the block of flats now. All the lights were out. She let the curtain fall back into place, tapped her fingers on the edge of the sink, and then went swiftly through to the living room and the front door. She snapped the lock and put the safety chain across. She felt immediately better, but scoffed at herself silently as she went back to the kitchen to dry the cup and plate.

She heard a car door thump down below and quickly pulled the curtain aside, leaning across the draining board to see out. The blue Holden's motor roared to

30

life, the headlights blazed, and the car drove off with a whine of gears, rapidly disappearing down the street.

Kathy blew out her cheeks and relaxed suddenly. But she wondered why the cup rattled so much when she put it on top of the plate.

Kathy couldn't believe that Patrick's body could be in such fine condition after three years in a coma. She was bathing him, on her second afternoon at the Roget Clinic, and as she wiped the damp cloth over him, she couldn't help noticing the tone of the skin, the firm springy feel of his muscles. He had a near-perfect body, tapering torso, narrow hips, long muscular legs. He looked better than some athletes she had seen in action and yet for three years he hadn't moved a muscle, had no food except the endless glucose drip nourishing him intravenously, plus whatever vitamin boosters they had given him.

She shook her head, slowly, taking a towel and patting his flesh dry.

"I don't know, Patrick, I really don't," she said quietly. "You are a real puzzle, aren't you? You've got us all confounded, one way and another. Most of all I'd like to know what is keeping you alive—if that's what you call your kind of existence. In fact, not only keeping you alive but keeping you fit." She put the towel aside and began to gather up the soiled bed-linen which she had changed earlier. She dumped it in the laundry bag and then ran a finger lightly down Patrick's unresponsive cheek. "You *seem* to be looking at me. I'd just love to get inside your brain and find out if there *is* anything going on . . ."

Kathy picked up one of his hands, it was limp, without response. Even a newborn baby will grasp at a finger, but here . . . nothing at all.

"Such a terrible waste, Patrick," Kathy said. "A beautiful body like yours and nothing inside it." She pulled up the sheet, tucked it in, and brushed a curl of hair away from his eyes. She glanced up at the gauges and dials and screens on the other side of the bed. There was a whole network of wires and tubes

31

connected to Patrick, monitoring his life functions. As usual, the needles were steady on the dials, no change. Not that she had been expecting anything else, of course . . .

"And how is our angry young man this afternoon?"

Kathy jumped a little and spun around. Doctor Roget came into the room, flicking her that quick-as-a-wink snaky smile, crossing to the bed.

"Oh, no change, Doctor," Kathy said automatically.

Roget gave her a straightfaced look and she flushed. He cracked another smile. "That's good, Sister . . . Jacquard, isn't it? 'No change.' If there ever *is* a change, I hope you'll come and tell me immediately!"

"Of course, Doctor." She felt herself flushing, knowing he was poking fun at her. "I've just given him his bath."

"Has he moved his bowels yet?"

"Not yet."

"Be sure to tell me when he does."

"Yes Doctor."

He moved to the bed, taking a stethoscope from his dust-coat pocket. He commenced to listen to Patrick's heart, but watched the monitor screen with the electronic graph. His face told Kathy nothing as he tucked the stethoscope away again and took out a penlight torch. He shone the beam into Patrick's eye and Kathy craned her neck to see if the pupil reacted to the light. She was unable to make up her mind as Roget leaned right over and looked into the other eye. His thumb and forefinger grabbed the eyelids and spread them wide. Kathy felt her teeth clamp together as she imagined the strain on the corners of the folds of flesh, she half expected them to tear. Roget was not exactly gentle with his patient and she found herself almost hoping that Patrick would spit in his face.

"He spits, you know," Roget said suddenly, straightening and Kathy started, thinking wildly for a moment that he had read her mind.

She started to speak but he flipped down the sheet and commenced drumming on Patrick's chest, tapping two fingers with the tip of his other index finger. "Mar-

32

vellous condition for a man who has been so long comatose. What do you think of Patrick, Mrs. Jacquard?"

"Well, I've had worse, I suppose."

"Indeed? I haven't."

Kathy had been vaguely aware of an approaching *clip-clop* outside in the passage and now the sound stopped outside room 15. The door opened and Matron Cassidy stood there, holding a square plastic container. She made no move to enter the room, in fact moved back a bit when Roget and Kathy looked up.

"Doctor . . ."

"Come in, come in, Matron," Roget said a little testily. But Kathy was sure there was a faint note of cruelty in the invitation too, though she had no idea why.

The Matron threw Roget a dagger-sharp look and held out the container, making no attempt to disguise her repugnance. "Your frogs have arrived."

"Good. Just put them down somewhere." Again that veiled sardonic note in his voice.

Matron Cassidy put the container on the laminex bench top just inside the door, then wheeled about and walked swiftly away down the passage, her shoes going *clip-clop, clip-clop,* almost cantering.

"See that?" Roget said, smirking.

"I beg your pardon?"

"The Matron. She won't come inside this room."

Kathy frowned. "Why?"

Roget shrugged. "Don't know. Got some queer idea that there's no air. Claims plants won't grow in here. You notice it?"

"Well, no."

"Me neither." He looked down at Patrick again, lying naked on the bed, a beautiful, sculptured figure. "Nor does he." Roget shook his head very slowly. "You know, I swear he actually seems fitter than when he came here eighteen months ago."

"Is that possible, Doctor?"

"On glucose drips? Hardly. But maybe we'll get to the bottom of the mystery one day."

Roget took up a small rubber mallet with a metal handle, lifted one of Patrick's arms, rapped him on the wrist several times, watching the fingers and dangling hand closely. No response. He tried again with the other hand and got the same result. Then he tried the elbows, the knees, reversed the mallet and pressed the metal handle's end against the soles of Patrick's feet, drawing it up from heel to toes. Still no response.

Kathy watched him as he moved about, apparently absorbed in what he was doing. He handled Patrick as if he were some demonstration cadaver in the students' lecture room, or like so much dead meat in a butcher's shop, ready for quartering.

"Why did you refer to Patrick as an 'angry young man,' Doctor?"

"Did I?" Roget asked, preoccupied with his probing and checking for reflexes.

"Yes. Was it because he came from Lochart?"

He snapped his head up, his bulbous eyes narrowed a little. "You ask a lot of questions."

"I was once told that a good nurse has an actively enquiring mind."

Roget returned to his prodding and poked at Patrick, leaving red marks on his skin.

"What did happen to him, Doctor?"

"Massive damage to the cerebral cortex."

"Yes, but how?"

"Some sort of electrical accident in a bathroom, the police said."

"The police?" Kathy exclaimed.

He looked at her steadily. "Yes. Some other people were hurt, I understand. Lend a hand, will you?"

Afterwards, as Roget scrubbed his hands at the sink, Kathy smoothed Patrick's forehead after tucking in the sheets. She looked at her hand sharply. There was a faint film of perspiration on it, but she couldn't be sure if it had come from her own palm or from Patrick's flesh.

Before she could think about it further, Roget said, still scrubbing, "The man is a bloody paradox. Eighteen kilos of dead meat hanging from a comatose brain and yet fit as an Olympic athlete! There must be some reason for it. When he was found after the accident, whatever it was, he was clinically dead. But through some 'miracle' of medicine and idiotic luck, they managed to restart his heart. And here's the result. Even if he could be somehow aware of what they had done, I doubt that he'd thank them for it."

"But you can't be sure that he's not aware of something." Kathy knew she was treading on dangerous ground, questioning a senior medical man of Roget's standing, but something impelled her to speak up. "I mean, there must be some reason why he spits."

Roget gave her a pitying smile. "Oh, there is. Let me show you."

She watched as he went to the container on the laminex bench. A number of mottled frogs clawed at the plastic walls, a sticky fluid from their bodies smearing the material. Kathy stepped back. She had dissected plenty of frogs, guinea pigs, even cockroaches, in Biology, but she hadn't liked it. The guinea pigs and cockroaches hadn't bothered her, but frogs . . . ugh!

Roget noticed her reaction, smiled crookedly as he opened a corner of the lid, reached into the container and lifted out one of the animals. It tried to leap away and Kathy was sure he deliberately pointed it in her direction.

"Are you watching, Sister?" Roget asked in a tone that told her she had better pay attention. He rummaged in his pockets and extracted a slim probe. He sank the probe into the base of the frog's skull, instantly killing it by severing the spinal cord. It hung limply in his hands, eyes still open, jaws agape, staring in her direction. A tiny bead of blood rolled into a corner of its mouth, formed a crimson sphere and then dropped into Roget's skeleton hand. He didn't seem to notice.

"Don't worry, Sister," he smiled. "Frogs don't feel pain the way we do."

How the hell do you know? Kathy thought, barely restraining herself from asking the question aloud. She felt sick, not because of the frog's death so much, but because of Roget's attitude. She decided then and there that the man gave her the creeps more than the frogs.

"Watch. I'll demonstrate for you exactly why Patrick spits."

He moved to a bank of instruments, carrying the dead frog and placing it on the bench. He took the defibrillator electrodes and removed one rubber pad. Adjusting the current as low as possible, barely getting a reading on the dial, he touched the electrode to the base of the frog's spine.

Kathy was unable to stifle the choked scream that rose into her throat as the "dead" frog leapt from the bench towards her and landed on the floor with a wet thump, skidding almost to her feet. Roget smiled, switching off the power.

"See? Pure motor reflex, reacting to a stimulus."

Kathy turned away in disgust.

"Oh, come now, Sister, we're not going all watery-kneed over a frog are we?"

Kathy got hold of herself but there was still a tremor in her voice when she spoke. "A reflex, reacting to a stimulus, you said. What is the stimulus that Patrick reacts to, Doctor?"

His face sobered and his eyes were hard, boring into her. "You do have an 'actively enquiring mind,' don't you? I suppose you think that makes you a first class nurse."

"No, I, I'm just eager to learn, Doctor."

He thought about that, tapping a thumbnail against his teeth. "They gave him all kinds of tests at Lochart, you know, even wrote him up in one of the medical journals. They tried monitoring him twenty-four hours a day with an electroencephalograph that registers *any* kind of brainwave activity—from a fart to a nervous breakdown. They had him wired-up to that machine for almost 1200 hours and you know what it registered? Just farts."

Kathy looked somewhat sadly at Patrick. "Then why not just let him die?"

Roget gave her a mirthless smile. "He is already dead. It's the machine that's alive. It does everything

36

for him, this complex we call the life-support system. It breathes for him, circulates absolutely pure blood, keeps him in a comfortable, stable environment. Supports—life, or what passes for it here."

"You could switch it off." Kathy gestured to the machines.

Roget frowned, reasoning half aloud. "I suppose there is every reason why we should. He doesn't have a family, nobody ever comes to see him. He takes up space, he costs the taxpayers a lot of money. He ties up all this expensive equipment twenty-four hours a day. Even Matron Cassidy argues it would be kinder to just allow him to slip away."

"What is your opinion, Doctor?"

"I'm a physician, governed by a Code. I don't need an opinion."

Kathy felt nervous now but she had taken the step and felt she had to follow through, even if Roget blew up and put her in her place—as he had every right to do. In fact, she was surprised that the discussion had gone this far.

"I'm sorry, Doctor, but I don't think that's a very satisfactory answer."

Roget looked up from wiping his hands on a towel. He had just dropped the dead frog into the waste bin. He was slightly annoyed now. "Then you shouldn't ask unsatisfactory questions, Sister."

Kathy knew that was it, she couldn't persevere now without getting herself into a lot of trouble. She may well have jeopardized her position already. Then, Roget turned and leaned his hips against the laminex bench, folding his thin arms and looking at her thoughtfully. She felt sure he was going to reprimand her. She couldn't possibly know that despite his aggravation, Roget liked to make his point, even with a junior staff member like Kathy. Patrick's survival and continued apparent gain in physical health, was a subject that fascinated him profoundly. It was the source of all his seemingly boundless energy.

"Look, Miss, do you really want to know why this miserable creature is kept alive? Why he rates several

37

hundred-thousand dollars' worth of equipment that could be better used elsewhere and why he has two nurses of his very own? Determining the exact moment of death is one of the most controversial issues in modern medicine. At what point does whatever it is that makes a person *live* actually depart the body? Eh?"

"You mean the soul?"

Roget made an impatient gesture. "Look, I'm a man of science, I'd prefer not to get bogged down in religious concepts. Let's stick to medical *facts,* Sister Jacquard. Now, the brain has billions of cells or working parts. You could feed it ten new facts every second for the rest of your life and still only tap a fraction of its potential."

"It's an extraordinarily powerful instrument that we carry around on our shoulders," Roget continued, his face intent, bordering on the fanatical now as he warmed up. "We can probe around and find the nerve that will make a patient wiggle his toes, get an erection, or scream in pain. We can make him laugh, convulse with pleasure, or knock him cold. Just by touching the right nerve. But we are still in the dark ages when it comes to the more sophisticated functions of the brain. What I'm after is possibly the most sophisticated function of all—the nebulous bridge between the conscious and unconscious, life and death." He shrugged bony shoulders under his dust-coat. "We could be talking about what Yogis call the 'Life Force,' Russians call the 'bioplasm' and Christians call the 'Soul.' Whatever *it* is, it's the single thing that seems to differentiate a living man from a dead man. You see, Sister, dying may occur slowly but *Death* occurs like the blink of an eye. You're either alive or, *zap!* You're dead!"

"Like the frog, Doctor?" Kathy asked dryly.

"Exactly like the frog! When did that animal die, hmmm?"

"Presumably when you sank the probe into its brain."

"Oh? Really? Not, perhaps a second later? A *split* second later? Or maybe it was the electric shock that wrenched this co-called 'Soul' or 'bioplasm' from the flesh. Could there have been an element of decision, the frog saying, "Well, this is it, I'm going to die—now!"

"Nobody could know that!" Kathy protested.

"Nobody *knows* those things, Sister. But, with careful, patient research, it may not be entirely impossible to find out. It may even be possible to establish a tangible link between the Natural and the Supernatural." He smiled crookedly, that flickering snake-smile. "Sufficient reason for keeping that lump of meat wired-up to those life-support machines, Sister, mmmm?"

"Then he's just a guinea pig to you?"

"Oh, far more than that. He is a very rare opportunity to study this grey area between life and death. Something in that fine specimen simply won't give up. It *lives* inside him, has done for three years. He is locked somewhere between life and death. With a little luck, I'll have *years* to study it, all the time in the world, all I need!"

Kathy was a little shaken by his vehemence, his intensity. More, she was a trifle shaken by the knowledge that she could almost condone Roget's experiments. What a break-through if he should be successful! And why shouldn't Patrick perform some service to mankind? After all, it was man's ingenuity and technological know-how that was keeping him . . . alive? No, suspended.

Somehow, when she chose that word, she knew she could never condone Roget. Who knew what kind of hell Patrick might be suffering, unable to communicate and let them know? It would be better if they terminated him.

"Let me know if—when—his bowels move, won't you, Sister?"

Kathy started at Roget's matter-of-fact tone as he picked up his container of frogs and went out, that smile flicking on and off.

Kathy sighed heavily and went to bed, smoothing the already smooth sheets, gazing down at Patrick tenderly.

"Poor devil," she said quietly, lightly running a hand around his jaw. "Poor, poor devil."

39

Chapter Three

Captain Fraser dragged himself down the corridor at a slow pace, his walking aid *tap-tapping* on the polished linoleum. He was wearing his Army coat and slouch hat as usual and his pyjama pants dragged on the floor, almost totally covering his slippered feet. He stopped at the sound of a door closing behind him. The old body almost creaked as he shuffled around, twisting stiff and rheumatic neck muscles.

Kathy was just coming out of Room 15, and, as she came down the passage towards him, she removed her cap and unclipped the badge at the throat. She smiled.

"Good night, Captain. Do you need any help?"

He cackled, but sobered abruptly. "Better lock 'im in tight." He jerked his head towards Patrick's door.

"Oh?"

"Yeah, flies out the winder sometimes of a night. I've seen 'im whizzin' past me own winder when I been watchin' for the Bosch." He leaned forward conspiratorily. "The Big Push is comin' soon. I reckon that bloke in dugout 15's a spy too. That's where 'e goes when he flies out the winder. Takes messages to the Hun. I'll shoot 'im down one night."

Kathy was trying to keep a straight face. "Well, it's good of you to spend so much of your time looking out for the rest of us, Captain. But you should get some sleep. You can't be alert unless you have proper rest." She took his arm, shocked at the thinness of his bones beneath the thick greatcoat material. "Come along. I'll take you back to your dugout."

He struggled to pull free. His eyes looked a little wild. "He's got somethin' in the wall, too. I can 'ear it. Tries to make me think it's rats, but I reckon it's a secret radio, I hear it hummin' an' clickin' an' fizzin' . . ."

"It could just be that old electric sign outside his window making those noises, Captain," Kathy said gently. "Now come along. Back to bed."

Captain Fraser went a couple of steps with her then stopped abruptly. Kathy turned to admonish him and noticed the screwed up face, the little-boy, mischievous gleam in his eye. Puzzled, she asked, "What is it?"

Then she smelled something, looked down in time to see a stream of yellow urine flooding out from under his baggy pyjama trouser cuffs.

"Oh, Captain Fraser! I could—shake you!"

He grinned with those dreadful, rotten teeth as she put on a severe face, sighing resignedly.

"Come along, I'll get you changed and cleaned-up before I leave."

Kathy's back and arms were aching as she strained to reach the high part of the wall with the paint roller. She was using a beautiful sky-blue acrylic that dried quickly and her face and hair were spotted with it. Some had run down one arm and dried to powder. Her old, cut-off jeans were stiff with it.

She felt dirty and tired and a little dizzy, perched on top of the tall kitchen stool balanced atop a coffee table. It was a scaffolder's nightmare and she was well aware that she was risking a bad fall, but she was determined to finish the paint job tonight. There were only the high parts to do, over in this particular corner, and then she would have completely painted the living room. She had decided against papering one wall to turn it into a feature and had instead painted it a darker blue. Once the framed prints were back up, arranged in thematic groups, and the new throw-rug she had splurged on yesterday was in the centre of the floor, it would be a very bright room.

Kathy was in need of some cheerful surroundings.

41

She put up a good front, but she was actually quite unhappy. Maybe it could be said it was her own fault, for she had been the one to walk out on her marriage. Ed had tried in his own bumbling way to make things work and God knew she had done *her* best, but something just didn't seem to click. It was like a jigsaw puzzle—almost perfect, except that one piece was missing.

She hoped she might find the truant piece by spending some time alone, away from Ed and his sexual demands, tasting independence and a certain freedom. So far, she had to admit that she was enjoying these things, but was no closer to locating the last bit of the puzzle. Maybe that was her mistake, maybe there were a dozen or more pieces missing—too many for her to ever complete the picture of happiness she had envisaged.

She was jarred back to the present as the stool tilted dangerously when she made a lunge for the final patch of the ceiling with the dripping brush. But the paint found its mark and she steadied herself, regaining her balance just in time.

"Well, I think I will take that as a warning," she murmured, gingerly climbing down from her precarious eyrie. "But luckily, that's it!" She stood back with hands on hips, ignoring the excess paint that oozed off the roller onto her leg, and admired her handiwork.

She let the roller plop into the paint tray and it splashed over the huge sheet of plastic she had spread out. The room was a mess with all the gear, but she was seeing it with the cane sofa and chairs in place, bright orange cushions, wine-coloured drapes, and the new multi-coloured throw-rug on the polished floor. Yes, she could live in this room and feel its cheerfulness, any depression here would be of her own making. Kathy stifled a yawn and stretched, arching her back, groaning a little. She would put the paint away in the morning, right now she needed a hot shower and then a good night's rest.

The silence was broken by the phone ringing. It was in the bedroom next to the bed, in case she was required at the Clinic. As she hurried through now, shoving the door with a random thrust of her arm, she hoped that Matron Cassidy wasn't wanting her to replace Panicale on the night shift. The little dark nurse with her cold had called in sick yesterday and Paula Williams had to take over her shift. Kathy knew it would be only fair to spread the inconvenience around and somehow, even while she was enjoying herself painting, she had had a nagging feeling that she was going to be recalled to the clinic.

"Hello," she said, forcing brightness as she spoke into the receiver. She started to sit down on the edge of the bed then remembered her stained shorts, so thrust a shoulder against the wall for support. "Hello?" she said again. She knew someone was there. The line had the hum of a connected number and she could vaguely hear something, sounds she thought she could recognize but couldn't quite discern well enough. "Hello!" she snapped. "Who's there? Ed . . . ? If that's you Ed, I'm going to hang up."

She slammed down the receiver and started untying her halter top, going swiftly out of the bedroom towards the bathroom, angry. If it *was* Ed . . . surely he couldn't have found out where she was yet . . .

She decided she was not going to think about it and by the time she had reached the bathroom she was naked, her paint-stained clothing scattered where she had shed it. The warm water did wonders for her aching body and she stood under the steaming stream deliberately making her mind a blank, soaking in it, allowing it to wash away the tensions and physical twinges. It was a baptism. She had now *really* started a new life for herself.

She had found herself a job, she had located this flat, she had painted the living room and would redecorate the rest in time. She was independent for the first time in three years.

It was a good feeling and she savoured it until the water started to chill and she knew the system's reservoir was running out of hot water. She dried herself slowly and dusted herself with perfumed talc. By the time she pulled on the white shirt she wore instead of a nightie, she felt more relaxed than she had done for months.

Sliding between the fresh sheets was pure pleasure and she decided to add to it by having one last cigarette before turning out the bedside lamp. She had almost finished the smoke, allowing the pre-sleep lassitude to slowly claim her body, when she thought she heard a soft sound from the living room. At the same time, the bedside lamp bulb flickered several times. Wide awake now, Kathy frowned, listening. Yes—there it was again. She was sure she had fastened the chain lock, but perhaps not . . .

Kathy pushed off the continental quilt, slid out of bed and crept into the living room. There was enough light from the streetlamp to allow her to see that the bracket of the chain lock had come unscrewed from the wall and was dangling ineffectively from the chain. Obviously she was better with a paintbrush than a screwdriver—she would do something about it to-morrow.

She headed back towards the bedroom. She stopped, aware that the bedside lamp was off. "Oh, hell!" she muttered, remembering the flickering bulb. "And I don't have a spare!"

As she reached the doorway she was grabbed from behind by a pair of strong arms and forced onto the bed. She started to scream and a nicotine-smelling hand clamped across her mouth, choking it off. She smelled beer and whisky on the man's breath as he panted over her. She struggled and kicked but he was far too strong. A hand ripped the buttons off her shirt and she heard the *zip* of his fly. She writhed violently and then caught sight of her attacker's face in the light coming through the window. She went limp, her arms flopped to her sides.

"When you're finished, Ed," she said in a steady voice, despite being short of breath, "I think we should discuss our divorce."

She felt him wilt almost instantly and he rolled off her, lying on his back across the bed beside her.

44

"Jesus!" he hissed, and she heard his fly zip up. He propped himself on one elbow, gazing down at her just as she lay, looking at him with contempt. "So much for women's rape fantasies."

Then, after her words had registered in his alcohol-numbed brain, he exclaimed, "Divorce? I thought this was just a trial separation!"

"It started out as a separation. Now it has progressed to divorce."

He was a big man, good-looking in a rough sort of way, and he towered over her as he stood up now. She wasn't afraid of him; he looked embarrassed, ashamed.

"Kathy, for Christ's sake! Jesus, I *care* about you! I want us to be together again! I was trying to do something about it!"

"You want to do something for me, Ed?"

"Sure I do. Just name it."

"Then get lost!"

He dragged down a deep, shuddering breath. "I see." He sounded more sober now, an instant transformation. "Look, Kathy, you probably don't believe me, but I *will* do anything you want—as long as you'll agree to give it another go."

Kathy's angry expression did not change, "Ed . . . The idea was for me to try to go it alone for a while. You agreed."

"I'll agree to anything that will make you happy, Kathy!"

"Then stop following me. Oh, I worked out it was you in that blue Holden the other night. It wasn't your car, but I knew it had to be you."

"I borrowed it from a mate. I, I'm sorry about the rape bit. It was stupid. I've had a lot to drink."

"Good night, Ed."

"Can't we talk about things, Kath?"

She walked out of the room to the front door and held it open, looking coldly at him as he stood in the bedroom doorway, dejected. He sighed and came forward slowly.

"You didn't think that lock would keep anyone out who really wanted to rape you, did you?"

45

"You mean you didn't *really* want to rape me, Ed?"

His lips tightened. "All *right!* Be bloody smart about it! Have a good laugh with the other nurses at that loony's clinic! You can drop bloody dead for all I care!"

He shouldered past roughly and Kathy closed the door, locked it and lent her forehead against the woodwork.

So much for feeling good, she thought. The mood had been well and truly shattered now. Just the same, she was glad it *had* turned out to be Ed.

"Well, I reckon it shows he *does* care for you."

Paula Williams shook out the sheet and walked around the end of the bed as Kathy held the opposite corners. They draped it over Patrick and Paula tucked it in under the mattress, while Kathy turned down the top and made it smooth over Patrick's chest.

"Care for me? By trying to rape me?" Kathy asked.

Williams looked at her steadily. "Let's face it, obviously sex was the reason your marriage broke up. Oh, don't look so shocked, it's a pretty common ground for conflict, so I hear. The way I see it, Ed was trying to do something about it."

They finished making Patrick's bed without any more conversation, then, Kathy said, testingly, "Why do you think it had to be sex that caused the trouble with Ed and me?"

Williams laughed. "It's always sex! I reckon if two people are happy in bed together, they're *happy!* That is my entire, unabridged, unexpurgated philosophy in a nutshell."

"A little too simple, I think."

"Look, Kathy, maybe I'm not one to be handing out advice because I've never been married. Played house a few times, but I never did have that little piece of paper that says my lovemaking is 'legal'—if you *can* legalize a natural function! But, anyway, I see it this way, you've got two choices. Get yourself a good solicitor, or a boyfriend."

Kathy frowned, staring down at Patrick without ac-

46

tually seeing him. His large blue eyes looked straight up at the blank ceiling as always. The drip bottles were still. The window was closed. For a few moments, the only sound was the quiet *pock-pock* of the life-support system. Paula made a cursory check of the gauges and monitors.

"I don't think I want either, Paula," Kathy said finally.

"You don't have to go as far as divorce. Get an injunction for him to stay away from you."

"Ed would ignore it!"

"Well I keep getting the impression he really cares for you, Kathy. Maybe you should unbend a little."

Kathy flashed her a look. "Not till I've had my chance at independence."

Paula lifted her hands out from her sides. "That could be where the boyfriend comes in . . ."

Kathy shook her head. "Not yet. Maybe not ever."

"All right. One more thing, you're coming to a party Friday night."

Kathy blinked at the sudden change. "I am?"

"Yes. Brian's parties are fun. It will cheer you up."

"I don't know, Paula, Friday's a long way off yet."

"Gives you time to think about it then. But I mean it, Brian turns on a terrific gig." She winked. "He could turn you on, too. He has that effect."

"Who is Brian?"

"*Doctor* Brian Wright. He's a neuro-surgeon. Really a bit of a dish, if you like the playboy type."

"Look, Paula, I appreciate what you are trying to do, but I don't want any involvements just now. Anyway, I'm in the middle of redecorating my flat."

Paula picked up the dirty linen bag and stopped beside Kathy as she started around the bed.

"Think about it, Kathy. And decide to come. You will have a good time. I'll guarantee it."

They moved towards the door and Kathy held it open for Paula. As the darker girl squeezed through with her bundle, Kathy smiled and said, "I'll promise to think about it. But no more. Okay?"

"That's a good start," Paula said as Kathy closed the

door and they walked down the corridor towards the lift. "Wonder if that damn lift's working today?"

In Room 15 the life-support machine *pock-pocked* and the needles flickered on the dials, the electronic scan of the heartbeat peaked and wavered rhythmically, at the usual low level of activity. A thin sheen of sweat glistened on Patrick's forehead. Suddenly the peaking rate increased. Just a little at first, two peaks appearing on its traverse across the dully-glowing screen where only one had been before. Then there were three peaks, building higher and higher up on the graph. The pulse rate dial flickered, the needle seemed to quiver before rising steadily from fifty, through fifty-five, sixty, seventy, eighty, ninety . . . The heartbeat scan lines were a whole series of waves now. There was a rising, thin whistling sound, an electronic beeping, needles on other gauges changed position . . . respiration . . . metabolism . . . *cerebral activity!*

But, though the read-out needles that normally would have marked the increased agitation on the graph paper jerked violently, they lifted a hundredth of a millimetre, just enough to clear the paper's surface so that nothing was recorded.

There was a slight rattling sound that was sustained for perhaps twenty seconds.

The the locked, iron-framed casement window flew open of its own accord.

Chapter Four

The rest of the week was a hectic whirl for Kathy. Bitten by the decorating bug, she snatched every spare moment she could to go into the city, browse amongst the shops in Collins Street and often make a wild purchase.

Somehow, in between this spending, which shrunk her small bank account to microscopic proportions at an alarming rate, she carried out her duties at the clinic and the added chore of typing for Matron Cassidy.

"You're doing well enough, Sister Jacquard," the Matron had told her, standing in the doorway of Room 15, avoiding even looking at Patrick and certainly making no attempt to enter. "You appear to have organized yourself into a workable routine. But we can't have our nurses sitting idle, so I will give you some typing from time to time. You did say you could type at your interview if I recollect correctly? Yes, I thought so. I'll have one of the wardsmen bring up an electric typewriter for you. God knows there are enough powerpoints in this room for you to find somewhere to plug it in."

"Yes, Matron," Kathy had replied neutrally.

The Matron had started to turn away and then swung back, frowning a little, pointing to the cyclamen plant in a handmade glazed pot on the windowsill. Just as she did, the electric sign outside buzzed and flickered on, the red glow from EMERGENCY reflecting into the room. Beyond, Kathy saw the grey clouds hanging low in the evening sky and she imagined Captain Fraser downstairs, shuffling back into the clinic through the main doors, his duty accomplished one more time.

"You've wasted your money you know, Sister," Matron Cassidy said, in regard to the cyclamen plant. "That plant will be dead in a day or two. Nothing grows in here." She looked around, up to the ceiling, where the fluorescent tube was flickering a little, her nostrils widening. "No air or something."

"I thought it might flourish near the window," Kathy replied.

Matron shook her head. "You'll get a nice glazed pot out of it, anyway. If you don't want it, after the plant dies, I would quite like it on my desk."

"I'll see how the plant makes out, Matron."

Matron was brisk again. "I'll send up the typewriter and stationery."

She had left abruptly and the electric typewriter had arrived within half an hour. It was one of those with a floating ball that carried all the typeface letters. Kathy soon mastered it, though she made a few mistakes, but later increased her speed. However, for some inexplicable reason, every now and then a letter would come out wrong. She would be sure she hit the "S" key but perhaps a "K" would appear on the paper. She put it down to the unfamiliarity with the machine, but it annoyed her having to make so many corrections.

Matron had been right, she had worked out a good routine with Patrick that she had tried to vary as little as possible. Not that Patrick would have noticed any variations, of course, but she told herself that Doctor Roget had claimed the life-support system kept Patrick in a stable environment. She didn't know why, but she felt that perhaps she could add to this stability by following a strict schedule each day. Maybe it added just a little to his—comfort?—well, hardly that. Roget would have scoffed, of course, saying that Patrick wouldn't know the difference. And maybe he was right, but Kathy knew that no one could be sure Patrick felt nothing at all, and it was not much trouble to do a few

50

things that would make life easier for him if he *was* more sensitive than they believed.

She sponged him and trimmed his nails, shaved him, cut his hair, lubricated his eyes many times daily to keep them free of the irritating dust that is normally removed by flicking eyelids, lightly dusted his body with Old Spice Talcum Powder instead of the anonymous clinic product and generally lavished a lot of care on him.

She didn't fool herself. She knew why she was doing it and felt somewhat selfish, for it was as much for her own benefit as Patrick's. Kathy was glad to have someone who needed her.

Paula Williams tended to scoff. Williams was competent enough in her own duties, quite a warm person in many ways, but she did no more than was expected of her. As soon as the shift ended, Williams was always the first away, claiming the shower, going out of the door still adjusting some portion of her street clothes, eager to be away and into her social whirl again.

"You know your trauma's showing, don't you?" Paula said to Kathy one night when she dropped some more papers in for typing. "Matron's compliments," she added, handing the papers over to Kathy.

Kathy decided to ignore the comment and only said, "Did Matron say when she wanted these?" Kathy waved the papers Williams had just brought in.

Paula sighed. "Soonest, I suppose."

She went out and Kathy sat at the typewriter holding the papers for a long, thoughtful minute. After a while she realized the typewriter's motor was humming and there was a very faint vibration coming from the carriage. She was surprised to find the typeface ball quivering a little, as if there was an electric current passing through it.

Yet, she hadn't plugged the machine in . . .

When Kathy relieved Panicale at noon on Friday, the little dark-eyed nurse sneezed twice before clattering out of the room. The drip bottles rattled in the breeze

51

coming through the window and Kathy frowned. She couldn't understand why Panicale didn't close the window when she was on duty here, instead of sitting in the direct draught with a cold like that. Kathy looked down at her cyclamen plant in the pot. She gave a small gasp of surprise.

There was a brilliant pink flower amongst the healthy sheen of dark green leaves. She frowned, feeling it gently. Strange she hadn't even noticed a bud last night . . .

Williams poked her head in later that evening, just as Kathy was applying fluid to the paper she had in the typewriter, swearing mildly.

"Crazy typewriter," Kathy muttered. "Everything goes along fine, then suddenly all the wrong letters keep coming out."

"It's only a symptom of the old joint," Williams said off-handedly. "The lift is out of commission again; the laundry is full of electrical bugs, no washing machines, ironing press won't heat up; lights keep blowing in the toilets. I'm inclined to agree with Captain Fraser for once: the place is full of gremlins."

Patrick made a quiet spitting motion, cheeks puffing. The two nurses were used to the occasional reflex now and barely glanced at him.

"You've decided to come to the party?"

Kathy blinked at her. "Party?"

"Doctor Brian Wright's gig. It's Friday."

"Oh Paula, I'm afraid I forgot about the party."

"You're coming! It will do you good."

"Well, I'm not sure yet . . ."

"See you when we come off duty," Williams laughed, starting out.

Kathy stared at the door after she had gone, chewing at her bottom lip. She looked down at her left hand, at the light reflecting off the narrow gold band of her wedding ring. She hesitated for a long minute. The life-support machine *pock-pocked* away, the electric sign outside the window hissed and fizzed, the drip bottles clinked. There was just possibly a slight increase in the heart activity read-out graph.

Then Kathy made her decision and took the wedding ring off, dropped it into her purse and snapped the lock closed.

As Williams had promised, it was a real swinging party. Paula seemed to know just about everybody in the big courtyard of the house with its floodlit swimming pool. It was a magnificent mansion-like place, fully restored inside and out. Even the swimming pool setting matched the Edwardian air and decor of the place, with small marble statues around the edges. There were vine-hung bowers and garden seats set in discreet, flowery alcoves around the treed grounds. Kathy thought the place must be worth at least a million dollars.

Doctor Brian Wright was a beautiful man, Kathy thought when Paula introduced them. It was the only word to describe him. Tall, solidly built, handsome, with very white and even teeth, stark against his deep tan. He was much younger than she expected.

Kathy was sitting by the side of the pool, dangling her feet in the water. She watched absently as Paula, topless, swam the length of the pool towards her.

"How are you making out with lover-boy?"

"Who?"

"Brian!"

"Oh, I haven't seen him since I arrived."

Paula gestured to the pool, with a laugh. "He's got his eye on you!"

Startled, Kathy turned and looked down. Brian was swimming about underwater at the deepest end of the pool, apparently lost in some dreamworld of his own. "What is he doing?"

"He's got underwater speakers, pipes in his favourite music: usually Stravinsky or something."

"Will you be all right to get home?" Paula asked, flickering her eyes in Brian's direction. "You know where my car is anyway."

"Yes, I'll be fine," Kathy said hesitantly.

"Well, look, my keys are in the car and you are welcome to use it."

Paula pulled herself out of the pool. "I rather fancy

53

I'll be away all weekend! See you Monday," she called over her shoulder as she hurried to join a young man waiting inside the house.

Kathy smiled as Paula and her man hurried away. She glanced back at a couple in the pool who were obviously making love in the water. Then there was a splash beside her and Brian's head broke the surface, his arms hooking over the edge of the pool near her feet. He grinned up at her.

"Come for a swim, Jacko," he said.

Kathy laughed as she shook her head. "I don't think so. It's late and everyone seems to be going. I'd better go too."

"Hell, not yet! The real fun starts when most of the drinkers go."

"Listen, Brian, I was going to talk to you about something."

"Fine. Come on in and listen to a few movements of the 'Rites Of Spring' "—he indicated the submerged speakers at the far end of the pool—"then we'll talk about whatever you like."

"Brian, I wanted to ask you about a patient of mine at the Roget Clinic. His name is Patrick."

"So you're looking after him now, eh?"

"You know about Patrick then?"

"Yeah, read something about him in a medical journal once. Hopeless case. Listen—you coming for a swim or not?"

"I've just eaten," Kathy stalled.

"Means nothing. Take your clothes off and come in."

"Why was Patrick at Lochart, do you know?" she forced herself to ask.

Brian didn't answer. He turned on his face and dived beneath the surface, corkscrewing, going right down to the underwater speaker, looking up and grinning as he conducted an imaginary orchestra as it approached crescendo. Kathy couldn't help but glance towards the couple making love.

She glanced back to Brian and frowned. He was spinning over and over, clawing at his face. Was he clowning? she wondered, or was he in trouble? She withdrew her legs from the water and walked along the side of the pool until she was near him.

Brian's body arched like a bow and then snapped closed in a tight "U," knees up against his chin. He seemed to be flung about wildly, cannoned off the sides. Kathy looked around wildly. There was no one. Just the couple clinging to each other in the water.

Then Brian seemed to surge to the surface and she saw his mouth drawn back in a rictus, his eyes bulging, wild, hands seeming to tear the water apart. His fingertips broke through and something seemed to hold him back so that he had to make a mighty effort to smash his head through into the air. He gave a choked, bubbling gasp, his face imploring. Kathy leaned far out, grabbed his clawing, thrashing hand and pulled him into the side.

He dragged himself out, flopping on the edge, gasping for breath.

"My God!" Kathy breathed. "What happened?"

He was shaking, breath rasping in his throat. It was a good half minute before he could speak.

"I guess you were right about eating and swimming," Brian finally said, laughing off the incident.

However, as he pulled his feet away from the now perfectly still surface of the water, he stared strangely down into the depths, as if looking for some hostile but invisible presence.

Chapter Five

The cyclamen flower was dead.

It was the first thing that Kathy noticed when she reported for duty in Room 15 at noon on Monday. She made a silent "Oh!" with her lips and crossed swiftly to the window, not looking at Patrick, so disappointed that the bloom had not flourished. She reached out her fingers and touched the petals. They looked almost bruised, as if someone had crushed the flower in an angry hand.

As she touched them, they fell apart with the dry rustle of paper, dropping to the earth mixture in the pot. Kathy sighed, lifted one of the wilting leaves. It seemed to have some remnant of life still in it and she went to the sink, filled a beaker with water, poured some into the pot around the roots.

"Come on, old plant," she said quietly. "You did it once. Prove Matron wrong and bloom again."

"You are wasting your time, Sister. I told you so, earlier."

Kathy spun towards the sound of Matron Cassidy's voice, flushing a little. "You could be right Matron," she conceded. "But there was a flower in bloom on Friday. See? Here is what's left of the petals."

Matron made no move to enter the room, standing in the doorway as usual, a folder of letters beneath her arm. "The rest of it will wither too. I have some more letters for you to type. You seem to be managing to fit them in quite well."

"Well, the typewriter's a bit temperamental at times."

56

"Aren't we all?" Matron said dryly and extended the bundle of letters. .

Kathy walked over and took them, started to say something about Matron never crossing the threshhold of Room 15 but changed her mind. As a matter of fact, Matron Cassidy not only never entered the room, but she avoided looking directly at Patrick.

"I'll leave you to it. May want you to stand an extra shift, too, Sister. Panicale's called in sick. Again."

"That will be all right, Matron. Thanks for the chance at some overtime."

"I would like those letters as soon as possible."

She turned and walked away down the passage and Kathy closed the door, set the letters on the small table beside the covered typewriter, and turned to Patrick.

"And how are you today, Patrick?" she asked brightly, re-arranging the sheet, smoothing a strand of hair from his eyes. "Did the weekend shift look after you? No, I see they didn't even bother to shave you! Probably didn't sponge you down either. Well, no matter. I'll do those things for you. But I had better get Matron's letters out of the way first. Do you mind?"

She found herself pausing, as if waiting for an answer, then made a "tutting" sound with her lips and uncovered the typewriter.

Kathy worked on the letters for almost an hour, swearing at the number of corrections she had to make. Then Paula Williams popped in and Kathy noticed she was sporting a new tan, still with just the flush of the sun in it. The skin would fade to a beautiful even gold, as usual, she thought. Williams really was a lovely looking girl.

"How was the party? Enjoy yourself?"

"Yes, I did," Kathy answered honestly. "I see you had your weekend away with your doctor."

"Phillip Island. The sun shone both days and he has a private sunning yard. I'm this colour all over." She smiled. "You get on all right with Brian?"

"Depends what you mean by all right. He wanted me to go skinny-dipping with him but he had a queer turn."

57

Paula nodded, frowning. "Yes. He turned up at the Island yesterday. He said he had been drinking and eating before he went swimming. Must have been a violent cramp."

"He seemed to recover all right."

Paula smiled. "He did, and he's interested in you. Came all the way down to the Island to find out your address and phone number from me."

Kathy arched her eyebrows, surprised.

"He'd like to see you again, Kathy. I think you could probably get something going there if you wanted to."

"Mmmm . . . He's nice enough, I suppose. Bit too sure of himself, though."

Paula laughed. "Of course he is! Anyway, I've paved the way, or at least prepared you if he calls. You could unwind quite a few of your tensions with Brian, Kathy."

"Or wind up with a lot more! Thanks for trying, Paula, but I'll just let things happen. Play it by ear."

Then she hitched her chair in closer to the table and flexed her fingers. "Well, Matron did say she wanted these as soon as possible so I'd better get on."

"See you, and think seriously about an affair with Brian. I think it will do you good." Williams waved airily and left.

Kathy sat staring at the typewriter for a time, not really seeing it, thinking about what Paula had said. Thinking about Brian Wright. Then she shook her head, sighed, and rolled a sheet of paper into the machine, preparing to type.

By mid-afternoon she had finished the letters and when she took them to Matron's office, she was handed a fresh batch.

"Sorry to turn you into a stenographer, Sister," Matron said with one of her insincere smiles, "but you are making such a good fist of this that Doctor Roget has asked me to have you type up some of his correspondence. I said you wouldn't mind, especially as you have the whole night to put in."

"Oh? Then you do want me to take Panicale's shift?"

Matron gave her a wider smile which made it seem

even more insincere. "You said you could use the overtime . . ."

The Matron had the correspondence half extended and Kathy had the distinct impression that unless she agreed to type it up she would suddenly find she wasn't working the extra shift. She took the bundle and forced a smile.

"Thank you, Matron."

She attended to Patrick's wants for a while: clipping his nails, shaving him, brushing and combing his hair, sponging him down, and patting talcum powder onto his body. She put a fresh oversheet on the bed, replaced the glucose drips and moved to the window to adjust it so the breeze didn't clink the bottles together constantly. She glanced at her cyclamen plant as she did so. She frowned, staring.

It was blooming again; a fresh, bright, almost luminous pink flower amongst healthy, glossy greenery.

"Well, if this isn't the strangest plant I have ever seen!" she said.

Then she returned to the life-support system, made a note of the monitor readings on the clipboard, adjusted Patrick's sheet once more, and walked back to the typewriter. She typed up the letters for an hour and was on the second last one when she began to make a series of errors. Kathy sighed, exasperated, corrected the mistake and began typing the line again. It was an officious memo from Roget: ". . . that all staff be advised to complete taxation . . ." But the last word came out "taxatjkln."

She muttered aloud, tearing out the sheet of paper and screwing it into a ball. She rolled in a fresh sheet but instead of commencing again, paused and placed her hands on the keys in the approved typing fashion. She could feel the faint vibration through them, no doubt from the tiny electric motor that activated them. Then she typed slowly and deliberately:

KATHERINE FAITH JACQUARD.

She nodded in satisfaction and began to type the standard sentence: "The quick brown fox jumped over

59

the lazy dog." But she froze, truly alarmed now. It came out:

"The quick brown fox jumped over lmnopatrick."

Bewildered, Kathy moved the space bar and, on a fresh line poised her finged above the "K" key. She tapped it gently.

The letter "S" appeared on the paper.

Looking puzzled, she tried again. She selected the "A" key. The machine typed "R."

She jumped up as there was a hiss and crackling sound behind her. She spun in her chair, saw a sudden red glow just outside the window as the EMER-GENCY sign came on. It was already dusk and she hadn't noticed.

"Captain Fraser strikes again," she murmured and hit the side of the typewriter. "And his gremlins seem to have struck this idiot machine!"

She stood up and moved across to close the window, quite a chilly breeze had sprung up with the sun's setting. As she turned away from the window, she idly let a finger trace along Patrick's jaw line, but swiftly snatched her hand back as he made a rapid series of spitting sounds. There was no spittle, just a rapid-fire puffing of his cheeks, expelling the air between pursed lips. Her heart hammered and she blew out her own cheeks.

"Phew! You scared me that time, Patrick."

As she made to turn away, he repeated the series of sounds. Kathy froze, coming back slowly, frowning. She stood looking down at him, feeling a little foolish at her sudden thought that Patrick was trying to gain her attention. Still, she slowly reached out a hand towards his cheek.

He made a single spitting sound.

Kathy jumped back. She seemed almost mesmerized now and her hand shook slightly as she reached out to touch his skin. Before contact, he made the spitting sound again. Kathy snatched her hand back and covered her mouth.

"Oh, my God!" she whispered.

She stood there, both hands up to her mouth now,

eyes staring down at him, as he began a slow series of spits, varying them—fast, slow, rapid, single. As if in a trance, she moved slowly around the bed. Her eyes went to the monitors. There didn't seem to be any change in the readings. Then her eyes returned to the motionless Patrick, drawn down there magnetically. Her heart thumping, the blood pounding in her ears, she swallowed, gathered her courage and said, falteringly,

"Pa . . . Patrick . . . Can . . . can you . . . hear me?"

He made a series of quick sounds with his lips and Kathy reached out a hand to steady herself against the edge of the bench. There was an abrupt and profound heaviness in her stomach. She rubbed herself gently at her tight abdomen, feeling her body break out in a cold sweat. She glanced towards the door. Should she get help? Matron? Roget? But what could she tell them? That she had made contact with Patrick? But *had* she? Her mind was racing like a film projector gone berserk, flooded insanely with sounds and pictures of all that had been done and said in Patrick's presence. And if all along he had been *aware* . . . !

"Good Lord!" she whispered, straightening and leaning towards the bed. "Patrick . . . ?" Was she imagining it or did he really seem to be listening intently? "Patrick . . . If, if you can hear me I want you to make that sound with your mouth. Once for yes, twice for no. Do you understand?"

Patrick made a single spitting gesture.

Kathy felt herself all knotted up inside, her chest seemed to be clasped in an iron band. "Was that . . . yes?"

Patrick made the sound again.

Kathy eased down onto the edge of the bed, shaking. She closed her eyes briefly, then opened them again, looking at Patrick, feeling the excitement starting to build inside her.

"Patrick. Do you know where you are?"

Patrick indicated yes.

"Do you know who I am?" Again, yes. "Can you see me?"

61

His lips made out two spitting sounds—no.

She reached out and touched his shoulder. "Can you feel this?" He seemed to hesitate before indicating no. Kathy moved back from the bed, hands to her temples, trying to think what to do. Roget had to be told, of course, but she couldn't go directly to him, even with exceptional news like this. There was a matter of protocol. Matron Cassidy would have to be told first. Christ, she thought, who cares who's told in what order? Just tell *someone!*

"Wait here, Patrick," she said stupidly and then ran from the room, down the corridor, almost knocking over old Captain Fraser as he returned from switching on the outside sign, past the other rooms, clattered down the stairs and headed straight for Matron Cassidy's office. She paused, tried to steady her breathing, smoothed down her uniform and generally got herself under control, as well as she could. She knocked and Matron's curt voice bid her enter.

"Yes, Sister?" Matron was at her enormous oak desk, and looked somewhat annoyed. She had been writing a letter and, judging by the fancy, flower-framed paper, Kathy thought it must be a private one. "You look very flustered."

"Matron. Could I . . . show you something please? In Room 15."

The Matron frowned. "You feel there is something in the room that I have not seen?"

"Yes! Please, Matron! This is very important."

Matron sighed and with bad grace stood up, taking time to cover her letter with a manila folder first. "Very well, Sister, lead the way."

Of course the Matron would go no further than the doorway. She stood there, looking somewhat defiant, arms folded, glaring at Kathy, not looking at Patrick.

"Well, Sister?"

Biting her lips nervously, Kathy looked from the still form under the sheets to Matron and then back to Patrick.

"Patrick . . . ?" she said tentatively, aware that

Matron Cassidy had stiffened slightly at her enquiring tone. "Patrick, Matron Cassidy's here with me. Show her what you showed me. Please!"

There was a long pause during which nothing happened, except the frown of disapproval deepened considerably on Matron Cassidy's face. Anger started to show exasperation. She did not even glance towards Patrick, merely directed her cold stare to Kathy who was feeling quite desperate now.

"Patrick! Please! I've brought Matron, for you to show her." Her voice trailed off as she realized she was not making contact. She began to feel very foolish. She looked at the icily glaring Matron helplessly. "He . . . he spits," she said lamely.

Matron Cassidy continued to stare, her face a mask of ugliness as the frosty anger narrowed her eyes and tightened her lips. There was no need for her to speak, she had broken Kathy with that terrible look. Then, for a moment, there was a touch of pity in her eyes before she turned abruptly and walked away down the passage.

Mechanically, Kathy closed the door and then flopped limply down onto the chair at the typewriter, staring at the sheet of paper still in the carriage. What a fool she had made of herself! Was she going crazy? She turned in the chair and looked at Patrick rather forlornly. She didn't notice the flickering needles on the gauges, or the increase in the heart activity monitor graph reading.

"Oh, Patrick!" she whispered. "Just for a little while there I thought . . ."

She jumped, spinning back to the typewriter as there was a brief, rapid firing of the keys. Kathy frowned, looking down at her hands, but she knew she had not touched the machine. Then she gasped as she looked at the paper. Underneath all the trial typing she had done was a new word:

SECRET.

She turned slowly to stare at Patrick, her mouth gaping, feeling the breeze from the open window chill the sweat on her pale face.

Chapter Six

Kathy felt almost as foolish now as when she had brought Matron Cassidy into Room 15 and Patrick had refused to demonstrate. But Doctor Brian Wright didn't fix her with a cold stare. On the contrary, his look across the small table with its candlelight and intimate supper was very warm indeed. Kathy knew that his mind wasn't really on what she had just told him about Patrick. He was going to do his best to seduce her.

"Well?" She knew she sounded impatient but couldn't help it. "What do you think?"

Brian drained his white wine, poured some more, then tilted the bottle in her direction. She shook her head, swiftly covering the glass with her hand. "I didn't know who else to tell."

"I guess I can allow myself to feel sort of flattered," he laughed. "But why didn't you come and see me last night? After it happened? Why wait a full twenty-four hours?"

"I had to work Panicale's shift last night for one thing. For another . . ." She shrugged.

"For another, you thought whoever you decided to tell would think you a nut-case. Right?"

She looked at him steadily. "Do you think so, Brian?"

He sipped some wine. "I have to admit it beats just about any story I've ever heard, regarding a comatose patient or otherwise, but I don't think you're crazy, Kathy." He reached across the table and squeezed her hand. She did not respond, but continued to study his

64

face carefully. "Tired maybe, with extra shifts, the typing chore, painting your flat, not to mention the nervous strain of your marriage going on the rocks."

Kathy withdrew her hand from his. "You did have a long talk with Paula Williams, didn't you?"

He smiled. "Why not? I'm interested in you, Kathy."

"I was hoping you might be interested in what I had to say about Patrick."

"I am! But I've never examined him myself. There isn't much I can comment on. Except, I think you must have somehow hit those typewriter keys yourself while you were seated at the table. You said yourself you were fidgeting, your fingers tapping the table edge. Perhaps you unconsciously put them on the keys."

"And typed SECRET?" Her voice was taut.

"Well you were thinking that you should have kept the whole thing to yourself, after Matron Cassidy put you down."

Kathy sighed, "All right, Brian. I have to admit nothing strange happened today when I was typing. The machine seemed to behave. In fact, the whole place seemed exceedingly normal. The lift worked, the laundry was functioning again, no lights were flickering, and Patrick never spat once!"

"There you are then." He stood. "Come into the living room and we'll have a brandy with our coffee."

"No thanks, Brian. You didn't need to go to all this trouble. But, if you don't want to discuss Patrick any more, will you tell me one thing first?"

He came around to stand behind her chair, his hands gently caressing her neck. "Anything, Kathy."

"All right. Is it possible that a whole team of medical specialists could be wrong? About Patrick's condition, I mean?"

"Good God, yes!" he replied at once and she twisted her head around, looking up at him, startled by his frankness. He laughed. "I'd be the first to admit the possibility. Most of the time we're just pissing on our boots."

Kathy stiffened, resisting as he tried to force her to turn her head back so he could continue to caress her neck. "I'd prefer to think we're helping the sick and injured."

"Helping them?" He gave up trying to turn her head, dropping his hands to her shoulders, gently squeezing them. "I consider it's a good day if I don't make them any worse."

"Oh come on, Brian! That's ridiculous coming from a top surgeon like you."

"Is it? You know, way back in the dim old days of herbalists and witchdoctors, a healer was a man who *healed.* Nowadays, he's a man with a diploma that *tells* everyone he's qualified to prescribe this or that or cut you open, but his biggest talent is one for tax concessions. I don't have any delusions about what I do."

He lit a cigarette, walked back to the table and poured himself another glass of wine. "I used to be right into crusades once, all for great advances in medical science, the betterment of mankind. But now . . . Well, I guess I'm just into money and believe it or not, my disillusioned beauty, that makes the whole damn thing much more logical."

"I'm sorry. I shouldn't have bothered you."

"So I'm a cynic, Kathy. Why does that shock you so much?"

Kathy started to reply, then sighed and shook her head. "I don't know. I'm not sure that it really does. It's just that I . . . Well, last night, for a little while, I *felt* I had made contact with Patrick. I've felt all along that he might be aware of *something,* that he couldn't be as dead as Roget made out and still be breathing."

"Well, as you said, no further contact today." He snapped his fingers suddenly. "Tell you what. This whole business of consciousness/unconsciousness is incredibly complex, but there has been some work done on auras. There may be some relationship."

She allowed him to take her hand and he led her out of the dining room and along a passage to a blank white door. He opened it and turned on the light.

Inside, she saw it was outfitted as a photographic darkroom. She hesitated, but allowed him to lead her in and then he began rummaging amongst some stacked cardboard boxes, slim affairs like those used for X-ray plates. There was a small, opaque glass viewing screen set into a lightbox on one wall. Brian switched out the main light and a red glow instantly replaced it. He seemed to be concentrating on finding something in one of the boxes. He apparently found what he wanted, walked over to the lightbox and switched on the fluorescent tubes behind the opaque glass screen. He slid what appeared to be a small acetate X-ray plate up beneath the clip but it was like no X-ray that Kathy had ever seen before. In outline, it resembled a leaf, but there were brightly-lit lines and rays of varying intensity emanating from it, not quite touching the sharp outline, but commencing just a fraction out from it. There was no blurring of the leaf's shape at all.

"This is what is known as the 'phantom leaf' effect, Kathy. It is an ordinary leaf from the garden, but photographed electronically by a method invented by a Russian scientist named Kirlian."

"Oh, I've heard of it. Kirlian photography." Then Kathy felt a vague stirring of excitement. "It's used to photograph the energy aura of various animate and inanimate objects, isn't it?"

"Hey, who's supposed to be giving this lecture?" He laughed briefly. "But that sums it up pretty well. It could be the biggest thing since X-rays were discovered, because it demonstrates that there *is* an energy body, a duplicate of the physical body, and that we can capture it and hold it on film."

He changed the photo, talking as he did so. "After I snapped the leaf, I tore it in two, discarded half and photographed it again. See?" He pointed to the new photograph. Around the undamaged part of the leaf, the aura lines were as brilliant as in the first photograph, but across the damaged part they were vague, only just discernible. "Even though damaged, the aura was still there, but a lot weaker."

"Could you photograph a person this way?" she asked.

"Yes. And that is what makes it all so potentially

important. It reveals enormous differences in energy states in individuals. So it could have practical application for the treatment of disease."

She turned to smile up into his face. "You don't sound now as if you're only in it for the money, Brian!" she chided.

"Well, maybe I'll get in on the ground floor with this stuff and make my pile," he quipped.

"It's all a bit sci-fi, isn't it?" she said.

"Eighty years ago, *X-rays* would have been sci-fi. Today's magic is tomorrow's science. Why, who knows? The photographs I have here of a person's fingerprint, before and after emotional shock, could well be actual photographs of the soul, or part thereof!"

She spun around, looking at him sharply in the red light. "The soul?"

"Well, life force, or whatever. The more I learn about medicine, Kathy, the more I am convinced that science and religion eventually merge."

"I wish Roget could hear you say that. Can I see these photographs of the aura around someone's fingertips?"

He slipped the photographs under the clips on the screen and Kathy peered closely at the wire-like lines wavering out from the black ovals of the fingertips where they pressed against the electronic plate. One photograph showed a great deal more activity than the other.

"I take it that this one is when the person photographed was in a highly emotional state?"

"Correct." She felt him move closer to her. "And the owner of the finger was me. Just shows how emotionally aroused I can get, eh?" Then his arms slid around her.

"Brian, please don't try to force things."

He stared at her thoughtfully, very sober. "Hmmmm . . ."

Sister Panicale dropped two stitches from her knitting and lifted her head rather fearfully, staring at the typewriter in Room 15. It buzzed faintly, the typeface ball seemed to quiver gently. She closed her eyes briefly and opened them slowly. Now the keys quivered. She blew her nose boisterously with a shaking hand, using the motions to look covertly at Patrick.

A very strange and sometimes frightening room this, she thought. She never liked working in here, rarely glanced at Patrick, avoided touching him if she could, merely recording the monitor readings as required. She crossed herself and tried to adjust her knitting. Long ago she had given up trying to solve the puzzle of how the window kept opening after she had closed it, why the light flickered violently at times and yet the electricians tested the tube repeatedly and it was satisfactory, how plants withered and died within hours of being brought in here—except, of course, for the cyclamen belonging to Sister Jacquard. It was a very strange room indeed and Panicale concentrated hard on her knitting when she was doing duty here, trying to ignore anything out of the ordinary. Like the typewriter and its buzzing now. It was plugged into the wall, but the machine was not switched on. There was no way that she was going to touch it. No way.

She started as the door suddenly opened and the blood drained from her face.

Doctor Roget came bustling in, carrying a black leather bag and looking excited about something. He went straight to the bench and began laying out instruments from his bag beside the autoclave.

"Give me a hand will you?" he said brusquely. "I want these sterilized and then you can help me prepare him for an examination. What's wrong with you? Been crying?"

Panicale was scrubbing violently at her nose with a sodden tissue. She sniffed. "No, Dogdor. Jus god a code."

"Speak up, girl!"

"I'b god a bad code!" she bawled, shivering a little and hugging herself.

"Well, why don't you close the window instead of sitting in a draught?"

Panicale glanced swiftly at Patrick, then back to the

annoyed Roget. "I do. Bud id keebs obening!" She quivered again.

Roget's lips compressed. "Don't be ridiculous . . . Oh, for heaven's sake, go and get an electric radiator or something. I'll put these things in the autoclave myself. And be quick!"

Sister Panicale practically ran from the room as Roget muttered something and turned to the bench. He unscrewed the clamps on the autoclave lid and checked the water level. Then he dropped the instruments in one by one. They clanged metallically. Patrick made a spitting noise but Roget didn't even look up as he clamped the lid on again and switched on the power. He tapped the gauge on top, saw the needle quiver and was satisfied that it was not jammed and that it would indicate the correct reading as steam pressure built up inside.

Roget moved around to the monitor screens and gauges, checking the activity readings on the dials closely. He stood looking at the heart monitor screen and the brain activity dial for quite a long time, deep in thought.

The autoclave started hissing and Roget turned to Patrick. The monitors seemed to slow almost imperceptibly and the "peaks" on the heart activity line flattened. Pulse rate flickered wildly. It was almost as if Patrick feared Roget. Feared and hated him . . .

Roget took a long thin needle from his pocket and began pricking Patrick with it, starting at his feet and working up. There was no reaction. The autoclave valve whistled shrilly and he hissed a curse as he went across to switch it off. He was returning to Patrick when Panicale came stumbling in with a bar-type electric radiator. Patrick made a single, violent spitting sound.

"Hurry up, girl!" Roget snapped as he resumed his examination, now working over Patrick's chest and down his arms.

Panicale nodded and hurriedly stooped in front of a power point, plugging in the radiator and switching it on.

Patrick made a series of savage spits.

70

Suddenly Panicale let out a brief but piercing scream as the radiator fused in a shower of sparks. For a fraction of a second, every needle on the monitor gauges shot clear across the dials, then dropped back to their usual positions.

Brian's car was a hand-built Jensen, metallic grey in colour, and it rolled silently to a stop outside Kathy's flats. He yanked on the handbrake and eased around in the bucket seat to look at her. She seemed a little sad, but smiled fleetingly.

"Thanks, Brian. There's no need for you to come up."

"Of course there is. I'll see you to the door." He smiled at her, kissed her lightly. "Cheer up."

She looked at him soberly. "I'm sorry, Brian."

His smile seemed more forced now. "Rubbish. It doesn't matter, Kathy."

"Believe me, it matters!"

"Well, you've got a lot on your mind. I realize your separation is pretty recent."

Kathy smiled again, more easily this time, and kissed him lightly on the cheek. "To think I started out the night just to discuss Patrick with you!"

Kathy sobered, frowning a little. "Not to labour a point, Brian, but tell me honestly, without any wisecracks, how could it be possible for Patrick to be like he is?"

"Like you *think* he is, Kathy," Brian said and immediately held up his hands when he saw her face tighten. "All right, all right. Sorry. Well, let's see. It's *possible*, I suppose, if you look at it this way." He moved around more comfortably in his seat. "We all have five senses, right? Sight, hearing, touch, smell and taste. If we lose one, we automatically compensate. Say a man loses his sight, then he instinctively develops a keener ear, a more sensitive touch and so on . . ." He paused and sighed, pursing his lips a little. "Now, Patrick has lost *all five* senses. He's cut off entirely and . . . Well, Kathy, if there *is* such a thing as a sixth sense his must be a beauty!"

71

She nodded slowly. "I can understand that, Brian. Better than anything else you've said or shown me. Yes, I think you've hit the nail on the head. Patrick has developed a powerful sixth sense, something beyond our comprehension."

"Perhaps, Kathy. I said it was *possible* . . ."

She started to get out and Brian reached across to open the door for her. He got out his own side and looked at her across the low roof of the car.

"I'll walk you to your door."

She didn't protest and he held her elbow as they climbed the stairs to her flat. He took the key from her, opened the door and reached around the frame to switch on the light.

Kathy gasped.

Her flat, so carefully and lovingly decorated, was a complete shambles. The walls were smeared with what looked like squashed fruit and vegetables. The drapes had been ripped down, the sofa cushions slashed, bottles smashed, the rug was a mess of food dye and nail polish.

"Jesus Christ!" Brian breathed. "It looks like the work of a madman."

Kathy clenched her fists, fighting back the tears.

Chapter Seven

Kathy's anger was still with her when she reached the clinic just before noon the next day. She was simmering, seething, in a sustained rage that she had never known before.

She was so intent on recalling every detail of the shambles in her flat as she hurried down the side street from the tram stop that she did not notice the bright orange Chrysler parked across the street from the clinic's gate. She didn't even notice the big man who got out from behind the steering wheel and waited for a break in the traffic so that he could cross on a line that would allow him to arrive at the gates just about the same time as Kathy.

Brian's first impulse had been to call the police but Kathy had stopped him, without explanation, angrily insisting that she did not want police intervention. Brian had been hurt by her vehemence and her refusal to let him help her straighten up the wreckage.

Kathy had been awake most of the night straightening things up as best she could.

"Kathy!"

She stopped dead in her tracks as she turned into the clinic gateway, turning her head and seeing Ed hurrying across the street towards her. Kathy's lips stretched into a thin line and she hurried on up the drive towards the big mansion-like building. She increased her pace as she heard his feet running along the gravel behind her and when she reached the foot of the steps beneath the unlit EMERGENCY sign, she turned as he grabbed her arm.

"Get the hell away from me, Ed!" she hissed, raising her handbag threateningly. "If you've got anything to say to me, do it through your solicitor!"

Ed reared back from the menacing bag but his face was angry as well as wary. "Christ Almighty! Take it easy will you!" He grabbed both her arms as she struggled violently, hacking at his shins with her shoes. "Shit! What the bloody hell's wrong?"

Ed released her arms and she started the stairs, but he jumped around and got between her and the door.

"Hold on, damn you!" he shouted and then, realizing where he was, abruptly lowered his voice. "Kathy, please, I don't know what's going on! All I know is I got a call from my solicitor and that he wanted to see me about an injunction or something. Now will someone tell me what I've done, or *supposed* to have done?"

"My solicitor has advised me not to discuss it with you," Kathy said shortly and tried to step around him. He blocked her again. She looked at him coldly. "Ed. There are wardsmen here much bigger than you. All I have to do is call one."

There was a faint clinking sound from above their heads and Kathy glanced up instinctively. She could see the drip bottles on their stainless steel stand just inside the open window of room 15 stirring in the breeze. Only, she realized through her anger, there was no breeze this morning . . .

"Call the bloody Army if you like," Ed told her. "But you're going to tell me first what the hell you reckon I've done."

Kathy glared. "I'm talking about last night, Ed, you know very well I am. Unless you were too rotten drunk to remember." Then her shoulders slumped. "Honest to God, Ed, I never knew you had such a sick mind! The attempted rape business I brushed off as a stupid, little boy prank, an act of bravado, almost. But . . ." Abruptly she started to sob despite her efforts at control and Ed's face straightened as he put a hand tentatively on her arm.

"Jesus, Kathy, what is it I'm supposed to have done, for Christ's sake?"

She looked at him with tearful eyes, rummaging madly in her handbag for a handkerchief. "Ed, that flat wasn't much, but it was mine. I spent hours, days, painting and decorating it . . . I just don't see how you could be so, so cruel."

Ed blinked. "I was nowhere near your flat last night!"

"Where were you then?" she asked, disbelievingly, dabbing at her eyes.

"Well I . . . well, all you need to know is I was nowhere near your flat. What happened to it, anyway?"

She lifted her head, fixed him with a deadly stare. "You're a bastard, Ed!" she hissed, then shoved past him, ran up the steps and went in through the big double doors.

He started after her, changed his mind, and gave a heavy sigh as he moved slowly back down the drive.

In the window above the electric sign, the drip feed bottles rattled furiously.

The tears had stopped by the time she commenced duty in room 15 but her anger was with her, resentment building up in her at Ed's denials. He must take her for some kind of a fool if he thought she would believe that he hadn't wrecked her flat. She was rather sorry now that she hadn't let Brian call the police.

In the room, she hardly glanced at Patrick, deeply concerned with her own troubles, wondering where it was all going to end. Hell, their marriage hadn't been *that* bad, really. They had spats like any married couple, over issues that probably weren't all that important individually, but over the years they had been dragged up each time there was an argument and had assumed much more importance than they warranted. Like her wanting a little more freedom. Ed was the old-fashioned Australian male who thought a woman shouldn't work after she was married. He felt it was the man's job to be the provider. He couldn't see that she needed to have some sort of life of her own as well. She was cooped up in the house all day. If she wanted to go anywhere she had to take a bus or train. She badly wanted a small car of her own and had offered to go out and get a job to pay for it, but Ed was adamant that one car was enough for them. They had fought and fought over this issue.

Then there was the bed. Ed was virile and demanding whether Kathy felt like making love or not. His aggressive, beery fumblings often killed any desire she might have had and he ended up by telling her that she was "frigid."

She had been pacing the room. Now, to try to get her mind off her troubles, she leaned over Patrick to adjust the sheet, deciding she would perhaps trim his hair again.

Patrick spat in her face, spittle spraying this time.

She reared back and such was her mood that she instinctively lashed out and struck him violently across the face.

"You bastard!" she hissed angrily.

She was immediately contrite at such a totally irresponsible act. It frightened her. She had been so pent-up, wanting so much to strike out at something, anything . . . She picked up one of his limp hands in hers, caressing the fingers and palm agitatedly.

"Oh, Patrick, I'm sorry, I'm sorry," she sobbed.

She pressed his hand against her face and held it there for a long minute. Then she looked up slowly, sniffing, taking out a handkerchief and dabbing at her eyes and nose. She looked at his face for the first time since she had hit him.

One side was all flushed and angrily red from her blow. A tear rolled slowly down the cheek.

Kathy's mouth dropped and she reached out a trembling hand to touch the tear, examining her wet fingertip. She sat on the bed beside him.

"You *can* feel!" she breathed.

Patrick made a single spitting gesture with his lips. There was no spittle this time. Obviously it meant yes.

Kathy studied him in amazement for a moment and then slid a hand under the sheet onto his chest.

"Can you feel that?"

A single puff of his cheeks and the small explosion of air from his lips.

Kathy slid her hand down further, onto his stomach. "That? Feel that, Patrick?"

He indicated yes.

Kathy placed her hand on his thigh.

"How about there?"

He spat twice. She slid her hand down to his knee and shin and toes, asking each time if he could feel. He indicated no every time. Then Kathy hesitated, drew in a deep breath and put her hand on his pubic area, touching his limp penis.

"Can you feel that?" she asked tightly.

Patrick made no sound but Kathy felt his response.

She smiled slowly. "You can can't you? You can feel there!"

Kathy abruptly froze, hearing a faint sound behind her.

"When you have a moment, Sister Jacquard!"

Kathy's knees were suddenly weak as she looked into Matron Cassidy's cold features as she stood just outside the doorway of Room 15.

Chapter Eight

Kathy was on the defensive as soon as she crossed the Matron's office, speaking even as she approached the desk where the older woman sat stiffly, regarding her stonily.

"He's conscious, Matron! Patrick's conscious!" Kathy said, aware of the note of desperation in her voice. "And he can *feel!* You saw him!"

Matron stared at her like she was some kind of filth. "What I saw, Sister, was a pathetically mixed-up woman, enacting a sick, depraved fantasy!"

Kathy felt herself blushing to the roots of her hair. She leaned forward intensely. "It wasn't what it looked like."

"Sit down, Mrs. Jacquard!" Matron barked, not taking her eyes from Kathy's face for a moment as she sat slowly.

Kathy closed her eyes, speaking almost vacantly, very softly. Almost as if she was trying to convince herself now, as well as Matron Cassidy.

"He *was* conscious! He *can* hear! He can *feel!*" She looked up desperately. "I slapped him and he *cried!* Doesn't that . . ."

Matron was outraged. "You struck a patient! What kind of unprofessional conduct is this you're admitting to?"

"He *cried!*" Kathy exclaimed, voice breaking.

"So will a fresh corpse, if the tear-ducts and lachrymal glands still function! It proves nothing—except how irresponsibly you have acted, Sister!"

"Oh, God! Why can't you believe me?"

"Believe what?" Matron asked contemptuously. "That every time that thing in Room 15 spits, breaks wind or gets an erection it's a sign he's conscious? Trying to communicate? I find that morbid, Sister Jacquard, *extremely* morbid!"

"He needs help!" Kathy cried, half rising, fists clenched.

Matron looked at her coldly. "*You* are the one who needs help." She withered Kathy with that terrible stare she was capable of calling up at any time, then continued in a quiet enough voice. "You have been in the nursing profession long enough to know that files on patients are strictly confidential."

It was a flat statement and Kathy, puzzled, nodded.

"Yet you took it upon yourself to go over the heads of both Doctor Roget and myself by inviting an opinion on the patient in Room 15 from Doctor Brian Wright of Southern General."

Kathy was startled to know that Matron had this information. "He was interested in Patrick," she said, lamely.

Matron scoffed. "Brian Wright is interested in only one thing and it has nothing whatsoever to do with the patient in Room 15, I can assure you!"

Kathy looked strained, her hands mangled each other in her lap. "What *is* this conspiracy to keep Patrick hidden away like some . . ."

"Do you believe in euthanasia, Sister?"

Kathy was taken aback somewhat by the casual tone used by the Matron. "I, I don't believe in *uncontrolled* mercy killing, someone running around with a hypodermic syringe full of morphine."

"But you believe in it in a passive sense! In allowing someone to die for his own good?"

Kathy dragged down a deep breath. "Well, I don't think anyone has the right to play God."

Matron gave her a pitying look. "Coming from someone who calls herself a nurse, that's rather pathetic. Nurses and doctors play God every day of their working lives. If they are not prepared to, they certainly should not be in this profession!"

79

Kathy tightened her lips. "You're saying, of course, that there is no God!"

"Of course there's no God! What a monstrous sense of humour he would have, *if* there was a God! Ask the millions of children who starve to death each year! Ask the victims of hit-and-run accidents, the old women who are raped by junkie kids, ask the patient in Room 15, Sister Jacquard!" She shook her head vigorously. "No. No God, no Justice, no Compassion! Only fear . . . So he lies there, month after month, year after year, because nobody, including myself, has the simple decency to switch off the machine and let him do what he should have done three years ago!" She leaned forward across the desk. "He is an embarrassment, Sister, a constant reminder to us that medicine can prolong death much more effectively than it can prolong life! So, if it appears that there is a conspiracy to lock him away, it is because the mere sight of him is offensive to us, reminding us of our own inadequacy."

Kathy felt her lip tremble and she nodded, shaken by the Matron's outburst. "I, I can see your point, but . . ."

Matron Cassidy went on as if Kathy hadn't spoken. "Then along comes Sister Katherine Jacquard. Not only do you jog our memories that Patrick is still alive, still human, you claim we have neglected him, don't even notice he has feelings." As Kathy opened her mouth to speak, Matron shouted her down, bullying her. "You intimate that you, a probationary sister, have discovered something in a couple of weeks that a team of specialists could not find in three *years!* And, as if that were not effrontery enough, you place both Doctor Roget and myself in a very embarrassing position by inviting an opinion from an outside doctor, then merrily proceed to slap and fondle the patient in a manner that should have you blacklisted from every hospital in the country!"

Kathy dropped her head, feeling drained, defeated. "I only wanted to help," she whispered.

"And so you shall," Matron said.

Kathy lifted her head instantly, frowning in puzzlement, bewildered by all these changes of moods and subject. "I beg your pardon, Matron?"

The Matron smiled thinly. "I am not going to sack you, Sister Jacquard. Frankly, I need every qualified nurse I can lay my hands on. But you are to be punished. And your penance is that you shall continue to be responsible for the patient in Room 15, and you shall demonstrate that I was not mistaken in hiring you by doing *exactly* as you are told, no more and no less. You will keep your nose clean, your mouth shut, and your *hands off!* Do you understand me, Sister?"

Kathy quailed, feeling ill, as she nodded jerkily. "Yes, Matron." Her voice was barely audible.

"Now get back to duty!"

Kathy nodded again and practically ran from the office.

Matron glared at the door for a while, then lifted a heavy jade paperweight in the shape of a dragon and took out some papers from beneath it. She flipped through them until she came to a form bearing the tab, "Jacquard." She turned the page and searched for a section headed "Remarks." Then she began to write swiftly: "Insolent and possible pervert." She filled in the date and then placed the paper back beneath the jade dragon. It slid a little off the pile so that it touched the polished wooden top of the desk, resting at an angle on Kathy's file.

Sometime later, Matron glanced up, annoyed, from an Administration form she was filling out in triplicate.

The jade dragon was vibrating slightly, rapping on the desktop. She covered it with her hand, feeling the minute movement of its millions of molecules for a second before it went cold and motionless in her grasp. She placed it centrally on top of Kathy's file sheet and made sure it did not slip off again.

Kathy felt so shattered for the rest of her shift that she hardly remembered getting through the remaining hours. Certainly she did not remember the long tram ride home, nor walking down the street to her block of flats.

Her mind was still on the day's affairs as she climbed the dimly-lit stairway, rummaging in her bag for the keys to her door. As she approached, jingling her keys on the ring a little as she sought the correct one, the door opened. She stopped dead, gasping.

Ed stood there, filling the doorway, hair hanging over his forehead, sweaty and begrimed, in old clothes.

Kathy's shoulder slumped. "Oh, hell, Ed, I can't cope with you! Go away!"

He grinned widely, stepping aside and bowed from the waist. "You don't have to cope with anything. Come on in and see."

Kathy, as if in a daze, stepped into her flat, wary of him, puzzled because he wasn't drunk as she had first thought. She blinked. The place reeked of fresh paint. The walls had been repainted, new cushions had been placed on the sofa, the splintered coffee tables had been replaced, new bulbs burned in the overhead lights, there was a new throw-rug on the floor.

"I haven't finished it all yet," Ed said, "but I'll get around to it. Had to knock off to get the dinner ready." He sniffed loudly. "Smell it? Tuna casserole."

Kathy merely stared at him as she sat down in a straight-back chair at the small dining table which she now noticed had been set for two. Bewildered, Kathy wiped a hand across her eyes.

"I don't understand," she said very quietly. "Ed, what's going on?"

"Not much. Just believe me, Kath, when I say I didn't do it."

She studied his face and her own features softened. "Ed, I don't know what to think. I've had one hell of a day . . ."

"Well, as I said, you don't have to worry about dinner. It's in the oven. As for the rest . . ." He swept his hand around. "I took the day off work and fixed it up. Sure was a mess! Oh, and I changed the lock on your door. Whoever did it won't get in again. It's a deadlock." He took some keys from his pocket and pushed them across the table towards her. "And there are the keys, Kath. All of them."

She took them mechanically, staring down at them, "Ed, I . . ."

"Look, I just want to prove to you that I had nothing to do with wrecking the place."

She looked at him sharply. "I might believe you more easily if you told me where you were last night, Ed."

"You still know how to rub a man up the wrong way, don't you?" Then he sighed. "Well, Kath . . . I guess I'd better own up . . ."

Kathy was suddenly inspired and surprised at the same time. "You were with a girl last night!"

Ed stared in stunned silence. "How did you know that?"

Kathy couldn't quite suppress her giggle. "You mean I'm right?"

"Yes, well you can laugh if you like. But nothing happened. I was too damn drunk, I guess. Fell asleep."

Kathy smiled, reached across the table and squeezed one of his big hands. "You know, Ed, I have had such a rotten day, I believe I am almost glad to see you!" Then she straightened her face. "Thanks for telling me about the girl."

He shrugged awkwardly. "Bit of a blow to the old ego, nothing happening. I mean, you know I never had any trouble before."

"Now you know what it's like when you can't turn-on just when you'd like to and then to be told you're frigid!"

He frowned. "Kath, I never knew it was like that with you."

"It's not so great being boxed-in and hung-up all day, then having someone smelling of beer and cigarettes start mauling you and expecting a star performance." She couldn't keep all the bitterness out of her voice, nor did she try.

"Well, I've decided to change, Kath. I'm off the drink and that's not just a hangover talking, I mean it. I'll have another go at giving up smoking if you want." He slowed down in his enthusiasm deliberately, gauging her response, giving her time to digest the facts.

"I don't know what went wrong with us, Kath, but I'd like to give it another go . . . No, I don't expect right away, but if I can prove to you that I'm prepared to change, that I'll stay off the drink and do a few other things, will you think about it?"

"What other things, Ed?" she asked non-committally.

He shrugged. "You name it. You know that little car you were always talking about? I'll get it if it will make you happy, Kath, and give you that bit of freedom you want."

Kathy studied his face closely, seeing, with a little start, that he was really sincere. He looked so intent, almost willing her to believe him, that she smiled faintly, and leaned across the table, giving him a swift kiss on the forehead. They looked into each other's eyes.

"Let's just start with the dinner, shall we, Ed? And thanks for fixing the place up."

"You believe me, don't you, Kath? I might be a mongrel at times, but I wouldn't pull a stunt like that."

Kathy smiled. "I believe you, Ed."

Suddenly the mood was more intimate than she had intended to allow it to become and she stood up stretching, deliberately breaking it.

"Have I got time for a shower before the casserole's ready?"

"Sure. How about if I scrub your back?"

She shook her head. "Let's not rush our bridges, Ed."

He sighed in deep disappointment as she walked across the living room towards the bathroom.

There was no nurse on duty in Room 15. Because Panicale was away and the rest of the staff had been called upon to do extra work due to other absentees, Matron Cassidy and Roget had conferred and decided that Patrick did not need a night nurse. At least, not beyond nine o'clock when Kathy finished.

After all, what was the sense? The life-support system was never switched off, it was checked regularly all day long and could be trusted to look after Patrick's minimal needs during the course of the night. Anyway, the clinic had been told by its accountants that it would have to cut down expenses and both Roget and Matron Cassidy saw this as one way to do it.

One of the other night staff could be instructed to look in once or twice during the night to make sure that everything was all right. It wasn't as if Patrick would be requiring anything.

Room 15, then, was in darkness from the time Kathy left, the only light in the room coming from the glow of the dials on the life-support system and the intermittent red neon light from the EMERGENCY sign burning outside the window. Occasionally, the drip feed bottles clinked together in the breeze. The only other sound was the quiet, constant *pock-pock* of the life-support unit.

Until around 10:30 when the night staff had their first tea break and congregated down stairs in the room set aside for them.

Then there was a faint buzzing and the hum from the typewriter on the table. It continued for about a minute as if warming-up and, in fact, did increase in intensity. Then suddenly, almost experimentally, the "X" key depressed, the typeface ball jumped and printed a single "X" on the sheet of paper that was already under the roller. After a pause, the "X" key depressed again. Then again, and again.

There was a rapid series of taps, like a stuttering machine gun, and a whole row of "X's" stretched across the paper. The roller jumped up a space. Another row of "Xs" was typed, then, almost as if the force doing this now felt more confident and able to manage the machine better, the pace increased and row after row of "Xs" appeared on the paper, line by line, rapidly filling the page.

Sweat beaded Patrick's face, trickled down from his hairline and dampened the pillow. The dials of the life-support unit registered wild readings. The "Xs" continued to rattle out then abruptly stopped.

Pock-pock, pock-pock. Only the life-support unit made any sound. But the needles on the dials and gauges were poised, as if waiting for something, or as if something new had grabbed Patrick's attention.

Kathy was looking much better as she came out of her bedroom now, fresh and scrubbed after the shower, wearing a summery, cool dress, the edges of her hair still damp.

Ed got up from the sofa and came across. "You look terrific!"

"Thank you! How's the dinner?"

"Be ready in a minute. By the way, who is Patrick?"

Kathy stiffened. "What?"

"Who's Patrick, a boyfriend?"

"How did you . . . ?"

Ed gave her a crooked smile. "While you were in the shower, someone named Paula Williams rang up and said to tell you that your boyfriend Patrick would be alone each night from now on, whatever that means!" Ed sounded jealous.

Kathy realized Paula had deliberately been enigmatic when she had heard Ed's voice. She decided there was no harm in going along with Williams' little joke.

"Oh, I know what she means, all right, Ed. Thanks."

"Well, who is he? What does he do for a living?"

"Mmmm . . . I guess you'd call Patrick a man of leisure."

"On the dole, you mean?"

"You could say that, I suppose. He lives off the Government."

Ed scowled. "He was probably the one who wrecked your flat then!"

Kathy frowned at Ed's words and started to say something but suddenly decided the joke had gone far enough.

"Well, never mind about Patrick, Ed. I'm starving."

Ed obviously made a wrench to change his mood but he managed it and his smile was only a little stiff around the edges as he went to the dining table and held out a chair for Kathy.

"Madam . . . ?"

Kathy smiled, came across and sat down.

"Would Madam perhaps like a drink with her meal? Wine? Cocktail?"

"A little wine perhaps," Kathy said gaily, going along with Ed, knowing he was planning to seduce her later.

"As Madam wishes."

He brought a decanter and two glasses and poured some wine with a flourish. They tinkled the glasses together and looked at each other over the rims.

"To us?" he suggested.

"To the moment, Ed," Kathy temporized.

They sipped and then Ed became the Head Waiter again and bowed, backing away from the table. "Now for the *pièce de résistance* . . ."

He brought in a steaming casserole dish from the kitchen, holding it in a pair of oven mitts, and set it down on the table. He peeled off the mitts as he bowed again.

"Now, if Madam would care to sample . . ."

"Ed!" Kathy exclaimed. "You didn't put down a heat pad! You'll burn the table!"

"Oh, sorry, Kath." Without thinking, he grabbed the casserole in his bare hands, lifting it off the table.

Kathy gasped, staring as he held it, and she grimaced at the sound and smell of crackling flesh. "My God, Ed!"

A little bewildered, Ed dropped the dish and it broke over the floor. The skin inside his palms and finger was burned off, leaving raw, oozing flesh.

The strange thing was Ed merely turned his hands over and stared down at the mess. "I didn't feel a thing, Kath," he said incredulously.

They stared at each other in amazement.

87

Chapter Nine

Matron Cassidy puffed up the stairs to the top floor of the hospital, looking angry. She paused, holding onto the railing, glancing about her. Nurses hurried about their business down the corridors, pushing trolleys, taking medication to patients. Two wardsmen carried a white metal box with coiled electrical leads down the eastern corridor.

Behind her, Sister Paula Williams made her own way up the stairs, carrying a huge bundle of laundry, followed by Kathy.

"Coming through, please, Matron," Williams called and Matron Cassidy stood to one side.

Williams paused, blowing out her cheeks and shaking her head. "That damn lift is out again!"

"Obviously," Matron snapped. "I have just been on to the maintenance people. Had one devil of a row with them. They didn't want to come until Monday week, but I've finally made them agree to send someone over on Friday. It's ridiculous that a hospital can't get some preferential treatment."

Williams groaned. "Oh, my aching legs! Friday? Well, you will have the fittest team of nurses and doctors in Melbourne, Matron." She grinned easily and Kathy was envious of the way she could handle Matron Cassidy. As she pushed past to go about her business she quipped, "One of these days, this whole darn building is going to be stuck between floors!"

Matron frowned after her and then glanced at Kathy as she started past her. "I have a very good friend who is Matron in Casualty at the Royal Melbourne, Sister Jacquard. I was speaking to her this morning on the telephone."

Kathy felt the tension growing in her and swore angrily at herself for letting Matron affect her this way. She noticed that the two men with the electrical machine were going into Room 15. "Oh?" she said, politely curious, to Matron.

"Yes. Your name came up. She told me there was an Edward Jacquard treated for third-degree burns to his hands at the hospital last night. She understood you had already given some very adequate first aid treatment."

"Yes, Matron. An accident. He picked up a hot casserole, not thinking."

"In his bare hands!" Matron was aghast at such stupidity. "Very bad burns it seems."

"Yes. He will be off work for a month."

Matron's face showed nothing as she stared at Kathy. "Reconciliation?"

Kathy flushed. "Not really. Just a discussion over a friendly meal."

Matron gave her a knowing look. "Of course. Seen Doctor Roget?"

"No, Matron."

"Well, he's certainly not going to be pleased about the lift. Carry on, Sister."

Matron moved off down the passage, looking in rooms as she went. Kathy hurried on to Room 15 and went in. When Matron looked into Captain Fraser's room, the old soldier was still in bed, with porridge and milk dripping from his chin as he slobbered over a bowl. He cackled as she wrinkled her nose.

"Tucker's gettin' better. Must've got a supply column through, eh?"

"Have you finished making a mess?" Matron snapped, and took the bowl from him, placing it on the food tray on the bedside table. "Look at you! Why can't you try to keep yourself clean? At least *try?*"

"The Push is comin', you know. The Hun's about ready. But so're we!" Then he lowered his voice conspicuously as Matron scrubbed rather roughly at his chin and the soaking front of his pyjamas. "That's if *he* ain't given the whole thing away!" He jerked his head towards the wall of Patrick's room.

Matron said nothing, long since tired of the Captain's fantasies.

"He ought be shot at dawn!" Captain Fraser continued.

Matron frowned. "Don't talk nonsense."

"No, really. He should be wiped out," Captain Fraser insisted. "He's got a Morse key in there. Heard it goin' nineteen to the dozen last night. Sendin' messages, he is. Alertin' the Hun. Someone's gotta do somethin' about 'im!"

Matron regarded him soberly as she straightened, then, almost involuntarily, looked at the wall, beyond which was Patrick.

Williams and Kathy finished changing the bedlinen and re-arranged Patrick, Kathy punching up the pillows and fussing around, making him comfortable.

"I don't know why you bother," Williams said, gesturing. "Hardly worth the extra trouble."

Kathy paused, glancing at her. "Just making him comfortable, Paula. He *can* feel, you know."

Williams sighed. "Let's not go into that all over again. But don't forget *you* feel things, too. Even if Ed doesn't!"

Kathy frowned. "No, that was very strange, him not feeling those hands when they were so badly burned. I guess they'll be hurting today."

"Going back to him?" Paula asked shrewdly and smiled when Kathy flushed as she looked up sharply.

"Nothing has been settled. I'm merely going to cook a meal for him Thursday night. He can't do much with his hands so heavily bandaged."

Paula smiled. "I'll bet he realizes that! Sounds to me like that dinner-for-two thing was planned to lead directly to the bedroom."

Kathy flushed a little. "Maybe."

"Disappointed?" Paula chided.

Kathy smiled. "Maybe, again."

Paula laughed. "Well, you've got two men chasing you now, Kathy. I think you should decide on one at least. Maybe both."

"You mean Brian? I don't know, Paula. I can't quite bring myself to . . ." She shrugged.

"Well, the trouble with Brian is, he's a user. It's an innocent kind of selfishness, highlighted by devilish good looks, not much tact, perfection in nearly everything he does—and enough money to pay for his failures. I think you should give him a fling though. I mean, Ed's out of commission, so to speak, for a while, and . . ."

"Paula!" Kathy cut in. "Let me make up my own mind, okay?"

"Just trying to help! But if you don't fancy Brian as a lover, now is the best possible time to move back to hubby, when he can't resist much and when you can do plenty for him, get things off on the right feet. I really think Ed is going to get you back one way or another. Or kill himself trying. If you *don't* make a decision soon, though, you could end up like the dear, dear Matron. Now that would be a fate worse than death, wouldn't it?"

Kathy watched her go and then turned to look at the new electrical machine the wardsmen had brought in earlier. No doubt it had been placed here on Roget's orders. She looked at it more closely, saw the coils of wire and, half-buried under them, electrode pads.

"God!" she breathed, glancing swiftly at Patrick.

She recognized the machine now. It was for shock therapy.

Doctor Roget had his mind on other things, as usual, and didn't react as Matron Cassidy thought he would when she told him that the lift couldn't be repaired right away.

"Bit of exercise won't do any of us any harm, I dare say," he said, watching his frogs in their glass case in his laboratory. He counted them, moved across to a desiccator jar where he had another frog. But this one appeared to be dead. As he removed the lid, Matron caught a whiff of cyanide and stepped back. Roget smiled as he lifted out the corpse. "All in the cause of science, Matron, and cyanide is very quick."

"You shouldn't leave it in the bottom of that jar," she said, quietly admonishing him, indicating the pale liquid in the lower section of the jar. "Suppose the cleaners knocked it over?"

"I'll flush it down the drain later, don't worry," Roget said, laying the frog's corpse out on a marble slab near a small accumulator with various wires and dials hooked up to it. He started to attach the wires to the frog.

"What are you doing now?"

"Mmmm? Oh, trying something new." He glanced up, apparently just remembering something. "For Patrick, eventually. And that reminds me, I'd like *all* the early reports on him. Lochart and prior to that, especially anything to do with his accident."

Matron looked a little shocked. "But going back that far would probably mean contacting the police."

"Very well. Use the clinic's name. I'm sure it will get us co-operation."

He turned back to his experiment, dismissing her.

Patrick didn't seen to want to communicate that day. Kathy tried several times, even deliberately selected single keys at the typewriter, hoping there might be some indication that what had happened the other night had not been of her own doing, subconsciously. But when she hit the "K" key, it typed "K"; "P" when struck, typed "P". The typewriter was behaving perfectly and she did not make a single error when typing up the paperwork that Matron Cassidy had left for her. She seemed to be getting more and more pushed onto her, but just at the moment she didn't mind. It kept her from thinking too deeply about her own problems when she had to concentrate on boring business correspondence.

She tried voice contact with Patrick during the day but there was absolutely no response. By the time night came around and Captain Fraser switched on his EMERGENCY sign outside the window, Kathy felt a little dazed, in a bit of a stupor, from concentrating so hard for hours at a time in an effort to finish all the paperwork.

She was beginning to wonder if, after all, she had imagined the whole thing with Patrick. No, she hadn't imagined it, but just possibly it could have been an incredible coincidence, his spitting just at the times she put the questions to him. And Matron had been right about the erection—patients, both conscious and unconscious, had them.

If it was only a coincidence, then it truly had been an incredible one . . .

Sighing, Kathy reached for another administrative letter and rolled fresh carbon paper into the typewriter. She yawned, stopped, sat back in the chair and rubbed her hands over her eyes. Before she started, it was time to check Patrick's monitors.

She took the clipboard and stood near his head, beside the drip stand at the window, feeling the breeze. She glanced at her plant; it was thriving and now had two blossoms. She looked out into the night, saw the headlights of a car pulling up in the street outside. The lights went out and, as she turned back to record the readings from the monitor dials, she cocked her head, listening.

Kathy wasn't sure, but she thought she had heard the temperamental lift motor start up. Shrugging, she began writing, noting what seemed to be a very slight increase in most of the readings, but no more than the normal variation that had been occurring lately.

Outside in the street, Ed Jacquard sat behind the wheel of the little car after switching off the lights, thinking. It was a small Triumph sports car, with the hood up now, several years old. It could do with a tune-up, a bit of paint here and there, but basically it was sound and would be reliable enough for all Kathy wanted until he was able to work on the motor himself.

He held his heavily bandaged hands in front of him.

93

They still didn't pain but they were damn awkward to do anything with. Neil, who had sold him the car, hadn't wanted him to drive it, but Ed had been adamant. He wanted to deliver this in person to Kathy. It had cost him more than he wanted to pay, but it was still a good deal and he knew this was the kind of car she had always wanted. He glanced down at the big bundle of flowers on the bucket seat beside him.

He hadn't realized just how much Kathy meant to him until she moved out. That wrecking of her flat had really thrown him. Whoever had done that had been really vicious. If he found out who it was . . . But it had shaken him, made him realize just how vulnerable Kathy was now that he wasn't around. He had taken a damn good look at himself then, remembering the debacle of the girl he had picked up and tried to make love to, figuring at the time, to hell with Kathy, he'd get it where he could. But it hadn't been that he was too drunk at all, he just couldn't stop thinking that he was cheating on her. When he realized it the next morning, he knew it was time to make a move, attempt to get her back.

It seemed he was hexed, or something. She had been really happy about his restoration of the flat and everything had been going along fine—until that stupid accident.

"Attacked by a tuna casserole!" he said aloud.

Well, maybe it hadn't been a total disaster. She had been very sympathetic and was going to cook dinner for him on her first night off.

But buying her this sports car was the real inspiration. This would win her over if anything would, prove to her that he was sincere in wanting her back and trying to be a different man, one who would treat her better.

He used his elbow to push down the door handle and climbed out, placing the flowers, with their note in the envelope tied to the stems with blue ribbon, on the bonnet while he fumbled the keys and locked the door. He pushed the keys into the envelope and picked up the flowers, going into the clinic's gate. He hadn't noticed he was parked under a "No Standing" sign.

There was no one at the desk inside and he didn't like to call out, this being a hospital. It all seemed very hushed and the lights were dim, in fact, flickering a little, as he decided he might as well deliver the flowers in person, with or without permission. He saw the lift doors and headed towards them.

There was a hum. The doors opened automatically, silently. He stopped, expecting someone to step out, but the lift was empty. Thinking there must be some sort of electric eye arrangement that opened the doors when anyone approached, Ed stepped inside and pressed button "2" with his bandaged thumb. He stood clutching the flowers to his chest as the doors closed with a heavy thud.

The lift lurched and began to rise slowly. The light in the roof flickered fitfully.

Kathy didn't know how long she had been typing. In fact, she wasn't sure *what* she had been typing. She stopped abruptly and ran a hand across her forehead. She was sweating. Her hand trembled a little. She felt strange. Sort of weak, almost like waking up from an anaesthetic, slightly disoriented, one step removed from reality.

As she rolled the paper from the typewriter she shook her head, glanced towards Patrick and the monitors. No change, she registered dryly. Then she turned to check the letter she had written for errors, her lips moving slightly as she read:

Mr. C. F. Cox
C. F. Cox P/L
5/390 Norwell St.
NORTH MELBOURNE

Dear Mum . . .

Kathy stiffened in bewilderment. "What!" she exclaimed huskily, unable to believe that she had typed that. But she read on swiftly:

95

In relation to your Invoice No. 25-339 for arterial catheters, ordered by this Clinic 11.11.77, we have to advise that . . .

. . . the bastard came on really strong, so I fixed him up. Ha-ha. In his own swimming pool of all places . . .

Kathy gasped, stared at the words, her head spinning.

"My God! I never typed this!" She spun swiftly and stared at Patrick. Her eyes went to the monitors. There was an increase in his heart activity. Pulse rate had climbed into the high sixties. She slowly returned to the words on the paper which now shook in her hands.

. . . Ed burned his hands but it served the bastard wright. Now he's the one who's all boxed-in and hung-up! Ha-ha . . .

The letter, if it could be called that, was signed "Your Loving Daughter, Kathy."

Shaking now, feeling sick inside, but determined to have it out with Patrick, Kathy stepped forward, dragging down deep breaths in an effort to control her thudding heart. Patrick's pulse rate was still climbing, towards 100 now, but Kathy didn't look at the monitors. She was staring at that handsome, blank face with the staring eyes, trying to will herself into whatever spark of consciousness still remained inside his head.

"I didn't type this, Patrick, did I?" she asked tightly.

There was no response from Patrick. Kathy felt as if her head was about to burst. She was close to reaching the end of her tether.

"*You* typed this! Using my hands! Didn't you?" she shouted. She moved forward as if to shake him but suddenly reared back as the windows flew open and closed shut in unison, then started opening and closing at random.

Patrick's demonstration lasted only seconds but Kathy felt her mouth sag, there seemed to be a lack of air, she couldn't breathe. She wanted to turn and run, but couldn't move.

The typewriter hummed loudly. There was a solid "click." She turned her head around. All the key tabs were depressed. The typeface ball was jammed up on its spindle, hard against the roller. As if in a daze, Kathy strode across, pushed the ball down. The key tabs rose to their normal position. Then depressed again and the ball jammed once more. Kathy pushed it back, seemed to shake herself, and reached for a sheet of paper, rolling it into the machine.

"All right, Patrick!" she gritted, breathing raggedly, hanging on to her sanity in the face of this. "I don't know what else you are capable of, but show me something on that paper! Send me a message! *Something!*"

Nothing happened. She was calmer now, determination making her jaw jut a little. "I'm going to outlast you, Patrick! I've got all night!"

Immediately, she realized the foolishness of this statement. Patrick had forever.

"I'll start it for you." She leaned over the machine and typed briefly. "Dear Mum . . . " "There you are. Now, Patrick, is that your mother or mine? It *can't* be mine, because she died when I was still a baby! So, it must be yours, Patrick! *Your* mother! Write something for her, Patrick . . ."

Kathy reared back, gasping, as the paper zipped up violently out of the typewriter and fluttered to the floor. She slammed her hand down in anger on the table, immediately rolled in a new sheet. This was going to be settled tonight, one way or another!

Then the lights flickered. The drip bottles vibrated and rattled together so hard that Kathy was afraid they would break. The windows opened and closed. She noticed that the cyclamen flowers were withered.

"Well, aren't we a clever boy!"

She whirled as the typewriter suddenly rattled and figures and letters appeared on the paper.

$$\frac{Pr+1}{Pr} = \frac{Kr^n + 1P^{r+1}Q^{n-r-1}}{Kr^n Prq^{n-r}} = \frac{Kr^n 1P}{Kr^n q}$$

97

Kathy looked dumbly down at the equation. "What is it?"

The paper flew out of the carriage and fell to the floor. Kathy's lips compressed as she rolled in a fresh sheet. Once again, she typed, "Dear Mum . . ."

There was no response from Patrick. Kathy stepped over to the bed, still breathing fast.

"Did you wreck my flat?" she asked between her teeth, going along with the realization that had been gnawing at her brain since he had started banging the window. *"Did* you?"

The drip stand started to fall and she caught it swiftly, set it up, holding on to it. Now there was anger breaking through, no longer subversive to the fear.

"Why are you doing this?" she hissed. "What . . . what is it you *want?"* Receiving no response, she picked up the "letter" and read aloud as she came to stand beside him. " 'Ed burned his hands but it served the bastard wright . . . ' With a 'W', as in Doctor Wright! I didn't type that, Patrick. And this bit about the swimming pool. How can you *know* this? Are you claiming responsibility for these things? Are you trying to frighten me?" She added, bitterly, "You're doing a damn good job if you are . . . Patrick? Please . . . Communicate!"

She felt herself winding down, being drained out, the fear coming back strong, twisting up her insides. Kathy put a hand to her temples wondering if she was going out of her mind.

If she wasn't, if these things were actually *happening* to her, why had Patrick suddenly decided to give her a demonstration of his powers? And just how much was he capable of?

Kathy slumped down at the table and slowly lowered her head onto her arms on top of the typewriter.

Chapter Ten

Brian glanced up from the "letter" and looked at Kathy: she thought there was a touch of—pity?—in his eyes.

"You say Patrick typed this?" he asked quietly.

"Yes!" Kathy snapped, then set down her coffee cup. It rattled in the saucer. She put a hand to her head. "He did, Brian! Using me, he typed that!"

Brian pursed his lips and blew out his cheeks slowly. He tapped the paper gently. "Mmmmm . . . This is getting serious, Kathy."

She stiffened, aware that she was in her dressing gown sitting across her breakfast bar from him, at eleven o'clock in the morning. She hadn't called him. He had come around of his own accord and she had decided to show him the letter and the equation—which he said meant absolutely nothing.

"You mean, you think I'm going out of my mind?" she asked tightly.

"I didn't say that, Kathy!" He smiled and closed a hand over hers.

"Well, maybe you're right!" she continued, still shaken up by what had happened in Room 15 last night. "Maybe everyone at the Roget Clinic was going out of their mind! It's odd, Brian! Roget and his damn frogs and his way-out ideas of treating Patrick, the latest of which appears to be shock therapy; Matron won't even enter Room 15; plants thrive and die; windows open of their own accord; the lights flicker wildly; washing machines won't work; the lift is jammed between floors again." She put trembling hands over her face. "It's enough to make anyone go crazy! And no one will believe me! Not Roget, not Matron, not you!"

Brian wasn't about to let this opportunity pass. He came around to her, pulled her out of the chair and folded his arms about her, the sympathetic figure.

"I am sure there's some sort of logical explanation for it all, Kathy," he said gently, stroking her hair. "I'm sure a lot can be put down to nerves, the pressures you are under . . ."

She stepped back, pushing his arms away, looking steadily into his face. "No! I damn well know it's not my imagination, Brian! Look, there's a term for making things move around the room without touching them, isn't there?"

He smiled crookedly. "Magic?"

She stamped her foot. "Damn it, don't make fun of me!"

He sobered quickly, held up a placating hand swiftly. "Okay! I'm sorry. The term is psychokinesis."

She calmed down. "There really is such a thing, Brian. I saw it last night. Have you ever seen it?"

"No—but I promise to keep an open mind. All right?"

Kathy nodded tightly and told him about the papers flying out of the typewriter, the windows moving, the drip stand falling. "All on top of the letter and that queer equation. Brian, I *know* I'm not crazy. But I will be if someone doesn't *believe* me! I *tried* to tell Matron. She offered me tranquillizers!"

She was shaking again and he pushed her gently back into the chair, handed her her coffee.

"Just what do *you* think is going on?" he asked gently.

She shook her head. "I don't know. But look at that letter. How did Patrick know Ed had burned his hands? Why spell "wright" with a "W" like in your name? The part about the swimming pool—that obviously refers to that queer happening there the night of the party."

He looked at her dubiously. "That was cramp, Kathy.

100

Swimming too soon after eating and drinking. That's all."

"It wasn't!" she insisted. "It was Patrick!"

"Look, Kathy, don't blame me if I seem sceptical. You can't lay something like this on me and expect me to agree with you right away—but I still have that open mind I promised!" He glanced at the letter. "What does this refer to? 'Ed's the one all boxed-in and hung-up . . .' Can you explain that?"

She shook her head. "No. Those terms were . . . I used them to my husband in a private conversation, right here in this flat. How could *he* know about that?"

"He couldn't, Kathy. He simply couldn't."

"But the words are there! You just read them!" She was getting emotional again, though she fought to remain rational. "By the way, did you mention anything about my asking you about Patrick? To Matron Cassidy, I mean?"

"Well, I did put out some tentative feelers about examining him," he admitted slowly. "Both she and Roget wanted to know my interest and I'm afraid I did say I had been speaking to you. Why? Trouble?"

"Yes. I was reprimanded for discussing a patient with an outsider. But Brian, I, I think you should examine Patrick. You're a neuro-surgeon. It might even be possible to use Kirlian photography to register his aura!"

"Now, wait a minute! That takes quite a deal of setting up. Besides, Roget won't allow me to see him."

Kathy looked at him steadily. "He wouldn't have to know."

Brian stiffened. "Good Lord, woman! I'd lose my job! It's not only totally insane, it's—unethical."

Kathy's mouth curled. "This from the man who claims medical science is pissing on its boots? *Ethics* already!"

"God damn it, Kathy! That's not fair! You don't understand my position! Patrick is Roget's patient!"

"You mean he owns him?" she snapped. "That he has the right to use him as a guinea pig for his crazy experiments? That he can pinch, and prod and probe and hook him up to electric shock machines just to see what happens? Is that *ethics*, Brian?"

He was sweating now. "Look, Roget is highly skilled, regarded as a top man in his field. God, Kathy, I simply couldn't . . ."

"No, of course you couldn't," she said in a suddenly deflated tone, but giving him a withering look. "It was just too much to expect."

"Look, if I could get permission . . ."

"You *won't!* They won't give you permission!" She sighed, "Brian, I'm not a fool. I know you only showed any interest at all in Patrick because it gave you an excuse to keep hanging around me—and I say that without any ego, I assure you. But I'll try not to hold it against you. I've intruded into your nice, orderly life, and I had no right to. I'm sorry."

"Christ!" he muttered. Then he sighed heavily. "How many staff on duty at night . . .?"

Kathy was running late and she hurried down the corridor towards Room 15, already shedding the light coat she had worn over her uniform. Brian had driven her in from her flat and she had been lucky not to run into Matron Cassidy so far.

As she approached the room, she heard a kind of dull, distant "thump!" and she frowned slightly, wondering what it was. Her hand reached out towards the the door handle.

"Tonight's the night!"

Kathy spun away from the door, heart hammering, spinning towards Room 17 where Captain Fraser had appeared. He cackled.

"Wh . . . what on earth do you mean?" she whispered.

"The big push is on tonight," the old man said, nodding emphatically. "The Hun's on the move. Gonna be some fireworks tonight, you see. So don't you go givin' anythin' away to that spy in there!"

He jerked his head towards Patrick's door. There was that dull "thump!" again from inside Room 15.

Kathy turned from Captain Fraser, opened the door

102

of Room 15 and stepped inside as the old man cackled again.

"Mark my words! It's on tonight!" Muttering, he turned and stumbled back into his room.

Kathy had moved just inside the door of Room 15. The "thump!" came again and she saw immediately what it was as Patrick jerked and writhed grotesquely on the bed.

Roget was applying the electrodes of the shock machine to his temples while Williams stood by the switch and voltage control. The dark girl looked up at Kathy but Roget didn't give her a glance as he moved the electrodes.

"Again, but increase the voltage two per cent," he said, "Quickly!"

Williams made the adjustments and threw the switch. *Thump!* Patrick jolted almost off the mattress, his eyes seeming to start from his head.

"Matron wants to see you," Williams told Kathy. "Right away she said, as soon as you came in."

"But . . . What are you doing?" Kathy stammered.

Williams rolled her eyes towards Roget who was muttering.

"Same voltage, Sister," he called, intent on holding the electrodes firmly for good contact.

Williams threw the switch and Patrick writhed. "She seems anxious to see you," she said to Kathy.

A little sickened, Kathy nodded slowly and turned away, closing the door after her and hurrying down to Matron Cassidy's office.

"You wanted to see me, I believe?" Kathy said as she entered.

Matron Cassidy looked up from some paperwork on her desk, gestured perfunctorily towards a chair. "Yes. Sit down, Sister Jacquard."

Ill-at-ease, Kathy sat down slowly, on the edge of the chair, hands folded in her lap, fingers tightly intertwined.

"You're late!" Matron observed. She held up a hand. "No never mind the explanations, I don't have time Sister. You will recall that when I hired you, it was

103

a condition that we would reserve the right to terminate your employment without notice."

Kathy stiffened, gave a puzzled nod. "Ye-es . . ."

"I'm afraid I will have to exercise that option. I would like you to collect your personal belongings and leave the clinic immediately."

Kathy was stunned. "But . . . why?"

"I never at any time indicated the position was permanent."

"No-o, but . . . Is it something I've done? Because I spoke with Doctor Wright about Patrick?"

Matron, surprisingly enough, began to fidget with the jade dragon paperweight. She seemed almost reluctant to sack Kathy, and yet, for some curious reason, was intent on doing it just the same: almost as if it were for Kathy's own good.

"The position was probationary, Sister," Matron said in clipped tones. "I'm sorry. I'll pay you till the end of the week so there will be no question that we haven't treated you fairly."

"Fairly! Matron, you can't just sack me without giving me a reason! You just can't!"

Matron toyed with the paperweight some more, then glanced up, her steely eyes meeting Kathy's. "Very well, Sister. I don't think you are cut out to be a nurse. Certainly not in this institution."

There was a short silence and Kathy was angry at herself as she felt herself close to tears. "What you mean is, it's because of Patrick, isn't it? I've stirred your conscience. Yours and Doctor Roget's! You think I know too much!"

Matron remained cool. "On the contrary, Sister Jacquard, I think you know too little. Even your typing has fallen off."

"My typing?!"

Kathy stood abruptly, very close to tears. "Really it is because I asked a second opinion on Patrick, isn't it? Because I spoke with Doctor Brian Wright! You don't want anyone else to examine him, do you? Roget wants him as his own exclusive guinea pig!"

"*Doctor* Roget, to you!" snapped Matron, becoming

angry now. "I had really hoped to avoid a confrontation, Mrs. Jacquard. I have a very full day. Please have the good grace to accept your notice and liberal pay and kindly—*get out!*"

"You can't do this!"

"The discussion is over, Mrs. Jacquard!" Matron stood abruptly, slamming the heavy paperweight down onto the desktop. She strode around the desk to the door, opened it and stood there glaring at Kathy, tapping a foot impatiently.

Kathy, tears welling up in her eyes, hurried out without another look in the Matron's direction. Matron Cassidy closed the door very firmly after her, expelling her breath in a long sigh as she shook her head slowly.

There was only Patrick in Room 15 when Kathy went in to gather her few personal belongings. Patrick seemed pale, but well enough after the shock therapy treatment, Kathy stood beside the bed, stroked his cheek gently.

"Patrick?" she asked in a voice with a catch in it. "I've just been sacked."

There was a sudden jerking of the needles on the dials and monitors. Kathy didn't notice.

"I've *got* to leave, Patrick," she continued. "Don't you care?"

There was no response from Patrick and Kathy smoothed his hair back from his forehead and lightly kissed it.

"I'm sorry I wasn't able to do anything to prevent Roget using the shock machine. I have to go right away. Matron wants me out of the place. I must get my things."

She went to the drawer of the desk and began to collect her few personal items. Then she jumped as there were four firm taps on the typewriter. There was paper in the carriage and on it the single word STAY.

She spun towards him. "I can't! They are literally throwing me out!"

The typewriter tapped twice. NO!

"I haven't any choice, Patrick! I'm sorry!"

105

She started to put her things into her shoulderbag. The machine rattled briefly.

HELP ME.

Kathy frowned as she stared at him. "How? How can I help you when you do absolutely nothing to co-operate?"

She waited, expecting a brief tattoo on the typewriter but nothing happened. She smoothed Patrick's forehead again. "What are you afraid of? Why don't you want anyone else to know you are aware?"

She waited but there was nothing. Sadly, she looked around the room, crossed to the window and picked up the cyclamen plant in the pot. It was blooming again and she was damned if she was going to leave that pot for Matron Cassidy. The typewriter suddenly began to tap. Kathy replaced the pot, walked to the table and read:

TRYING TO KILL ME.

Kathy was incredulous. "No they're not, Patrick. They think they're helping."

The typewriter rattled savagely. NO. GOING TO KILL ME!

"Who?" she asked desperately.

There was no response.

"Well, when?" she amended, and leaned forward swiftly as the keys rattled briefly.

TONIGHT.

Chapter Eleven

The frog stiffened like a starched puppet as Doctor Roget touched the thin electric wire to the tiny electrode taped to the reptile's head. All four legs shot out straight, locked in position at the joints. He touched one with his fingers, tried to bend it. It resisted, like steel. Roget twisted his mouth and took the leg in both hands, bending, straining, until it cracked and flopped uselessly. His eyes went swiftly to the small graph and needles he had hooked up to the implanted electrode.

It registered a sharp, angular peak with a violent jerk, and was then still. He smiled and switched off the current, picking up a rag to wipe his hands. When he turned, he started a little at seeing Matron Cassidy standing behind him in the laboratory, looking disapproving.

"What are you going to do?" she asked oddly. "Break the limbs of the patient in Room 15 to see if anything registers?"

"Don't talk nonsense!" Roget snapped, his good mood disappearing abruptly. "That frog had been subjected to a series of electric shocks, about twelve hours ago, just like our friend Patrick. I detected a small amount of increased cerebral activity a little earlier—see?" He lifted one end of the graph paper and showed the Matron a series of wriggling lines that had been traced by the electronic pens. "Not much, admittedly, but seeing the frog had been comatized over a period of days with repeated applications of anaesthetic, I find it encouraging."

Matron made no attempt to keep her disgust from showing. "Just what do you hope to accomplish? Surely there is nothing that the patient in Room 15 can provide for you now, Doctor? You have tried everything."

He smiled crookedly, a strange glint coming into his eyes. "Yes, perhaps I have now. But this time I may have some success. You see, Matron, I am treating Patrick with the cause! He was electrocuted, so I am giving him shock therapy. Who knows what results it may produce?"

She frowned suddenly. "Just what did happen to him?"

Roget seemed off-hand, checking some figures on a pad beside the dead frog. "It seems his mother, another man—lover, I suppose—and Patrick were all electrocuted in a bathroom. The police won't say for sure whether it happened when he was trying to rescue them, or if . . . he caused it."

Matron looked startled. "You mean . . . murdered them? Is that why he was at Lochart? They thought he was a homicidal maniac?"

Roget shrugged. "The police won't admit anything, because they had no *proof*."

"That's the kind of *thing* you want to put life back into?"

"He is a challenge, Matron! And I feel that I am up to meeting that challenge. I sent for you by the way because I want a nurse to stay with him all night."

"But we just decided to discontinue night duty because of costs!"

"I take responsibility. I have Patrick hooked up to the electroencephalograph. I want someone to sit with him all night in case there is some delayed cerebral activity, as in the case of our friend the frog here."

"I could only switch Panicale, Doctor, at this late time—if I can contact her right away."

"Not the ideal choice, but she will have to do if there is no one else available." He started perusing his figures on the pad again, glanced up at the Matron, frowning. "Well, please contact her! I want someone to watch that graph!"

Matron sighed heavily. "I have never said anything before, Doctor, but in the light of what you have told me about the patient in Room 15, I feel I must protest. I think he should just be allowed to remain as he is. Or to . . . die!"

"This is my clinic. He is my patient. I could well be on the verge of a break-through." His eyes were glittering, a little wild. "Please get that nurse on duty as soon as possible!"

Matron flushed, obviously shaken by his attitude and tone. She nodded curtly, turned and hurried from the laboratory. Roget went to his glass case of live frogs and selected another specimen, muttering quietly as he made some mental calculations.

Kathy eased open the basement door and peered in cautiously. It was pitch dark and she felt Brian close behind her; he was trembling a little. She didn't feel exactly relaxed herself but she was determined to go through with this, determined to make Brian live up to his part of the bargain.

Of course, then she would have to live up to hers.

She groped behind her for his hand. The palm was sweaty. "Stick close to me. We can make our way around the walls to the service stairs."

He pulled back. "Kathy, this is crazy!" he whispered.

She spun around. He couldn't see her face but he knew it would be set in angry lines, judging by her tone. "Brian, don't you dare pull out now!"

"God, it's so—unethical!"

"All *right,* damn you! If you haven't got the guts for this, we'll call it off right now!" she hissed, adding, coldly, "And just sit by and let them kill him!"

"Jesus!" he breathed and she heard him sigh. "Go on. I must be insane!"

Kathy said nothing, grabbing his hand and stepping into the big basement. He closed the door after him and the air felt thick and humid. There was a humming sound, accompanied by faint clicks.

"What's that?" he asked.

109

"Switchboard, I suppose. Emergency generator's down here, too, I think. Keep left. There's a . . ."

There was a sudden sound followed by Brian's swift barely-smothered curse. Then they both leapt back as a cascade of water flooded across the floor. A plastic bucket rolled dully and a mop handle clattered on the concrete. Their hearts were thudding.

"What the hell did I knock over?" Brian gasped.

"Mop bucket," Kathy whispered, recovering from her shock. "I was about to tell you to watch out for it. It has been placed there because the floor basin tap leaks. There's a short hose attached, which has probably come out of the bucket now. Watch you don't trip on it."

They skirted around the area, slopping through the water a little. Brian's shoe touched the hose and he kicked it aside. The movement jerked it up and out of the floor basin and let it rest on the edge where it trickled its small stream of water onto the floor to join the spreading pool from the bucket. Kathy stopped long enough to stand the bucket and mop against the wall, wanting to get out of the basement as quickly as possible. Somehow it gave her the creeps. Her nerves were on edge anyway and she jumped as some relay clicked over on the electrical switchboard with a solid sound.

Then she found the door to the service stairs and eased it open very gently. Dim light came in and Brian saw her pale face in the shaft, gleaming with a thin film of sweat. She opened the door wider, glanced up and down, and then turned to him, face grim:

"Ready?"

He nodded, still wondering what the hell he was doing allowing this girl to jeopardize his whole life this way. Marvellous what lengths a man would go to, just to get a woman into his bed . . .

Following Kathy, he stepped out of the basement and made his way slowly up the service stairs behind her, carrying his black instrument bag.

The clinic was quietly alive with the normal night-time noises as they made their way up around the brick wall that enclosed the lift shaft. As they paused at a corner, Kathy looked around cautiously to make sure the stairs were clear, Brian cocked his head, ear against the brick wall. Kathy turned to motion him on, saw his listening attitude.

"What is it?" she breathed.

"I don't know," he said frowning. "Sounded like banging and I thought I heard a very faint voice. What's behind this wall?"

"The lift shaft. But it hasn't been working. Perhaps the maintenance men are in."

"At this hour?"

"I don't *know!*" she hissed. "For God's sake, Brian. Let's concentrate on this!"

He nodded jerkily and indicated she should lead on. They moved around the corner and climbed the next flight of stairs to the floor above. They stopped at the top, the corridor dimly lit with only the night-lights.

"Where is his room?" Brian asked, tensely.

"At the side, towards the rear." Kathy started to move into the corridor and then stepped back swiftly, flattening against the brick wall, her face white.

"What is it?"

Kathy looked at him with wide eyes. "Matron. Coming this way with the desk nurse!"

Brian turned and bolted down the stairs.

Kathy began to tell him to stay put, still flattened against the wall. She should have reacted as fast as he did. Now it would be too late for her to move without the noise attracting Matron Cassidy or the nurse. If they came down the service stairway she would be . . . Kathy pressed so hard against the bricks she thought she must leave an impression on them.

Matron and the nurse stopped just at the head of the dark stairs, only a few feet from Kathy.

"I'm going home now," Matron said. "Remember to tell Panicale when she arrives that Doctor Roget wants even the *slightest* change in the monitors reported to him immediately. She is dense enough at the best of times but seems to be worse since she has had this cold. Make sure she understands."

"Yes, Matron—is something wrong?"

Matron was frowning as she stared at the service

111

stairwell, looking a little distant. "Eh! No, no, I was just . . . thinking of something. You go back to the desk, Nurse. And make very sure Panicale goes directly to Room 15."

"Yes, Matron." The nurse sounded a little puzzled but Kathy heard her hurrying away down the corridor.

Matron Cassidy still stood near the top of the stairs, her shadow on the wall opposite Kathy. She saw the Matron turn and look back down the corridor. She couldn't see Matron Cassidy's face. If she had been able to, she would have been puzzled by the expression on it as the Matron looked towards the door of Room 15. Matron's lips were compressed and there were muscles knotted along her jawline. Her hands clasped together in front of her, so tightly that the fingers were white and bloodless. It was as if she was steeling herself to do something.

Woodenly, Matron Cassidy walked over to the door, put her hand on the knob and let it rest there. Then, seeming to straighten with determination, she opened the door and stood there on the threshhold, looking at Patrick lying under the sheets, the electrodes and harness of the EEG unit connected to his head. Matron started to breathe a little faster, tensing herself, trying to will herself to step into the room.

She couldn't. She stepped back swiftly, closing the door after her. She wiped a trembling hand across her eyes, and rubbed her sweating palms together. She jumped as Captain Fraser poked his head out of the room next door.

"It's on tonight!" he cackled. "Death and destruction. Fire an' fury. Tonight's the night! The Hun's on the move!"

Matron shook herself visibly and went towards him with a grim expression. "Captain Fraser, if you don't stop . . ."

He closed the door in her face. Her first impulse was to open it angrily, but she stopped, and, looking strangely despondent, walked slowly back down the corridor. She paused by the service stairwell, then quickened her pace, her shoes *clip-clopping* away towards the main stairs.

Kathy released a sigh of relief, then started at a sound below her on the stairs. She smiled slowly as Brian came towards her, looking sheepish.

"It's all clear," she said to him, a little bitterly.

"Let's get on with it then!" he snapped and Kathy led the way swiftly to Room 15 and inside.

"Good God!" Brian breathed when he saw Patrick and turned down the sheet. "The man is a Mr. Universe!"

"And that is without exercise, just on glucose I/V drips," Kathy said rather triumphantly. "Do you see now what I mean when I said there was something strange here?"

"There certainly is," Brian said, a mild enthusiasm coming through now as he swiftly opened his bag and took out a small pencil light. He started to look into Patrick's pupils, raising the eyelids not much more gently than Roget.

"I don't know how much time we've got," Kathy said. "Panicale's on her way back. They must want a night nurse with him for some reason. I think it's to watch the EEG."

"See if you can communicate with him," Brian said, looking puzzled and very thoughtful as he continued to stare at Patrick's physique. He switched off the nightlight. The dials glowed eerily and Kathy leaned over the bed, "Patrick?"

There was no response. She exchanged a look with Brian, then stroked Patrick's cheek, pushed his hair back into place as well as she could beneath the EEG headband.

"Patrick—This is Doctor Brian Wright. He *knows* about you. What you can do. He wants to help."

There was still no response and Kathy felt mounting desperation as she foolishly shook him gently by the shoulder.

"Patrick! Please!"

Brian was tense, on edge. Discussing Patrick and his doings with Kathy had been one thing, but actually

113

seeing him, being here, clandestinely at that, *with* him, was a different matter altogether. He made swift and expert appraisals of Patrick's muscle tone, but could get no reflex responses, no change on the monitor dials.

Kathy was very edgy now. She went to the door, inched it open a little and looked out. "How long is this going to take?"

"How the hell do I know?" Brian replied. He looked at her steadily. "This was your idea. Don't rush me now that you have finally got me here."

"But I don't know how long before Panicale arrives!"

He sighed and put down his stethoscope. "I'm getting nothing. See what you can do again."

"How? He's not going to do anything! He wouldn't when I brought Matron, but I thought it was because he hates her—is maybe even—afraid of her. But because you are trying to help, I thought he might respond."

"See if you can make him get an erection again."

Kathy's jaw gaped. She felt herself flushing. "Are you serious, Brian?"

He merely looked at her. "We haven't got all night!"

Plucking up courage, Kathy sat down on the edge of the bed, hesitated, then put out her hand and grasped Patrick's penis. There was no response.

"Fondle him!" Brian hissed.

Feeling very self-conscious, Kathy tentatively did as she was told. Nothing.

She looked around at Brian.

"All right. Try slapping him."

Kathy gasped. "Oh, no! No, I couldn't, Brian. Not now that I . . ."

His mouth tightened as he pushed her aside and struck Patrick savagely across the face, loosening the head harness a little. Kathy put her hands to her face, expecting—what? Violence from Patrick? A tear?

But there was nothing.

Brian hit him again. Still nothing.

"Brian . . .!"

He looked at her coldly. "Seems a waste of time, doesn't it?" he gritted.

114

"No! You just said he has magnificent muscle tone and physique, both things impossible, or seemingly so, in a comatose patient! How about Kirlian photography? His aura! That would tell us something."

"I didn't come prepared to do that. Heavens, you would need a furniture van to bring in everything. But maybe you are right. Maybe the aura would give us a clue of some sort. Nothing else I've tried here seems to work . . ."

He broke off abruptly and stared at the EEG graph paper. Kathy looked around sharply and caught her breath.

It was registering a small degree of brain activity. Then the needles jerked violently and a wild peak of intense agitation, or stress of some kind, scratched across the graph paper.

Matron Cassidy halted abruptly at the side gate of the clinic, frowning as she stared across the street at the two cars parked there. One was Brian's metallic grey Jensen sedan, the other an old Triumph sportscar. There was a parking ticket beneath the windscreen wiper of the latter vehicle.

But neither car registered on Matron's mind. There were other thoughts swirling around in her brain, which felt suddenly lethargic, almost as if it was winding down after a heavy day, preparing to give itself up to the demands of the body for rest. In fact, her mouth opened as if she was beginning to yawn, but then she blinked and closed it again, actually giving her head a violent little shake in an effort to clear it.

A homicidal maniac in the clinic, she thought. It gave her the shivers just allowing the idea to consciously form in her brain. And Roget, the fool, was intent on trying to instill some sort of life into him. It was wrong. Completely wrong. But it had become an obsession with Roget now. He was stubbornly determined to strike some sort of response from Patrick, find out *why* he clung so tenaciously to life, come to grips with this mysterious "force" that held Patrick in limbo . . .

Matron put a hand to her forehead, surprised to

115

realize she was sweating. She somehow did not feel at all well. Her fingers plucked at the metal-framed glasses dangling around her neck on the gold chain.

Somebody had to do something.

As the thought shaped itself and gathered substance, her head turned robot-like, almost in slow motion, and she looked up at the window above the red EMERGENCY sign. The sanguinary neon glow reflected off the metal drip-bottle stand in Room 15. She continued to stare, registering that the night-light seemed to be out, and yet there was *some* sort of light moving about in there.

Sweat began to trickle down her face, chilling on her neck. Her fingers toyed irritably, unconsciously, with the spectacles. She felt so strange, dream-like, aware and yet not *quite* aware.

It was almost like the first insidious haze of unreality that crept over the body after a few drinks began to take effect. Pleasant, langurous, yet just beyond her control.

Her thoughts became confused. Roget and his frogs and the electric shock treatment. Jacquard, poking her nose in where it wasn't wanted, stirring their consciences, reminding them of the obscenity in Room 15. Patrick, some kind of monster that ought to be . . .

Matron shuddered, feeling sick. Then, trance-like, she turned completely about and walked woodenly back up the path towards the clinic.

"What does it mean?" Kathy hissed, watching the jerkings of the pens on the graph paper rolling out of the EEG.

"I don't know," Brian whispered. "He seems agitated."

"Well, you slapped him very hard!" Kathy admonished.

"Hmmmm . . . I have a feeling it is something more than that."

Kathy glanced at her watch, turning it so she could read the dial in the faint glow from the monitor screens and Brian's penlight.

"Brian—we haven't got much time."

"I want to see this," he said, throwing the torch beam onto the graph paper. "It's got to mean something!"

The needles jerked and scribbled, no longer aimlessly, but in seemingly meaningful peaks and hollows.

Kathy bit her bottom lip nervously.

Matron Cassidy had no idea why she skirted the lobby, moving silently, wraith-like, avoiding the reception area. She seemed to be aware of things only in flashes of clarity. She could not recall walking back up the path and reentering the clinic, yet she knew she had done those things. She was now walking in her stockinged feet, carrying her heavy shoes that normally *clip-clopped* along the corridors and alerted nurses and patients alike that she was on patrol.

She had no idea why she had removed her shoes, or when.

Matron found herself in the corridor leading to the big, silent kitchen. It was very quiet back here. Her stockinged feet whispered across the polished linoleum. Sweat was beading her face, soaking through the blouse under her arms. The spectacles bounced against her chest on the chain. Suddenly, she stopped, pressing back into the darkness, standing near the top of the basement stairs and looking back across the lighted lobby. Nurse Panicale was signing in, sniffing as usual. The little dark nurse scrubbed furiously at her red-tipped nose as the desk nurse gave her instructions regarding the EEG unit in Room 15.

The Matron leaned down and placed her shoes carefully on the floor at the top of the basement stairs, freeing her hands. As she straightened, she grabbed at the wall for support. Strange this light-headedness that was affecting her. For a moment, she frowned, looking around her, regarding her stockinged feet with a puzzled expression, almost as if she was trying to remember why she was here.

Then, seeing, and yet not seeing Panicale hurrying towards the main stairway leading to the floors above,

Matron opened the door and slowly started down the stairs into the basement.

The door closed silently behind her of its own accord.

The graph needles were kicking violently now and in the dim light Patrick had a kind of maniacal look to him. Kathy was frightened, not just of being caught, but by the way he looked. There had been no actual change of expression, and yet there was a madness in this room. She could feel it. She grabbed Brian's arm.

"Brian! We *have* to go!"

He continued to frown at the graph paper, then glanced towards Patrick. He didn't seem to notice anything different.

"Do you *want* to get caught?" Kathy asked, wondering how she could have been so stupid as to even propose this.

Brian sighed and started to gather up his things, putting them into the bag. He looked at Patrick again.

"You are a very interesting fellow, Patrick. I will definitely be back to study you some more. I'll get around Roget somehow."

Kathy opened the door slowly and froze. Panicale was just visible as she neared the top of the stairs. Then the dark little nurse sneezed and the motion made her drop her knitting and she stooped to pick it up, went back down the stairs, chasing the bouncing and rolling ball of yarn.

Kathy and Brian went out swiftly into the passage, closing the door of Room 15 gently after them.

"She will see us before we get to the service stairs!" Brian whispered.

"In here!" Kathy said swiftly and pulled him into Captain Fraser's room.

They stood just inside the door and almost leapt out of their shoes as the Captain cackled from his bed.

"It's on!" he shouted. "Told you it would be! The Hun's on the move!"

Hearts hammering, they waited, straining to hear sounds out in the passage over the Captain's crazy ravings. They could just make out the sounds of Panicale's shoes as she shuffled by quickly and then opened the door of Room 15 and went in.

They wasted no time in getting out of Room 17.

"There'll be death tonight, mark my words!" Captain Fraser croaked after them.

Out in the passage, Brian looked at Kathy. "Out through the basement again?"

"No need," Kathy said indicating her watch. "The desk nurse will be doing her rounds. The lobby will be empty. We can go out through that door."

"Then let's go before I need a change of underwear!"

Panicale settled herself in the chair near Patrick's bed, avoiding looking at him directly, sorting out her knitting. She glanced at the window, saw it was open. She knew it was no use closing it, but swiftly put the thought from her mind; she didn't want to think about the queer things that happened in this room.

She glanced at the EEG graph paper. It was blank.

There was a steady *drip-drip* somewhere over to Matron's left as she groped her way across the dark basement. She jumped a little as her stockinged feet stepped into the pool of water. She gasped at its cold touch and it seemed to jar her out of her lethargy, briefly.

What on earth was she doing down here?

Funny, she was just standing in the water, feeling it soak her feet. She really ought to step out of it and . . . *Why wasn't she wearing her shoes?*

Matron Cassidy put a hand to her head. She must be coming down with a virus. She didn't feel quite—right.

She was still struggling with the thought when she began to walk slowly across the basement towards the wire cage that screened the main switchboard and fusebox. A big sign glared at her on the padlocked gate: DANGER—HIGH VOLTAGE.

Matron stopped in front of the cage, breathing steadily, but stertorously. She fumbled in her pocket and brought out a leather key pouch. Holding it up to the dim light, she sorted through the keys and selected

119

a stubby one. It fitted the heavy brass padlock on the wire gate and turned smoothly. There was a slight buzzing, a humming sound, the clicks of relays as various equipment throughout the clinic was switched on and off through automatic circuits. The gate creaked as she swung it open and she stared a little glassily at the rows of switches and circuit-breakers. Her eyes moved around the big board and stopped on a huge prong-like switch with a black, heavily-insulated handle. Beneath it was a plastic plate with MAIN SWITCH engraved on it.

Matron Cassidy gave a brief, crooked smile as she shuffled her wet, stockinged feet closer to the board, reaching for the big, black handle with a trembling right hand, an out-of-focus look in her eyes.

Then the metal-framed glasses leapt out and upwards from her chest and clamped magnetically across the gleaming brass terminals of the main power inlet. Invisible arms seemed to clamp her to the switchboard. There was an instant shower of sparks, a violet-blue flash of light, an umbrella-shaped eruption of molten copper—and the abrupt sizzle and crackle of frying flesh.

Panicale gave a terrified gasp as the lights went off abruptly and plunged Room 15 into total darkness. The neon sign outside the window had also gone out with a fizzle. Panicale whimpered as she stood up, dropping her knitting.

She groped for the wall switch and flicked it up and down several times. Nothing happened. Panting, she stumbled to the door and opened it.

The corridor, the whole clinic was in total darkness.

Sister Panicale began to shake as she turned back into the room, her eyes going unwillingly towards the bed and the dark shape of Patrick.

Then there was a series of clicks, a muffled and distant mechanical coughing, and the lights began to flicker and waver again, building up from a dull glow to a steady whiteness.

Breathing a sigh of relief, Panicale closed the door

and turned to look at the bed again, feeling much more confident in the light.

She felt her heart stop in sheer terror.

Patrick, the man who had been in a coma for three years and who had not moved so much as an eye muscle in all that time, slowly turned his head a full ninety degrees on the pillow and glared maniacally at her.

She fell in an inert heap on the floor.

Chapter Twelve

The phone rang in the bedroom and Kathy snatched it up swiftly, glancing to see if it had wakened Brian, who was lying on his back beside her, gently snoring.

"Yes?" Kathy whispered. "Paula? . . . Do you know what time it is?" looking at her clock which showed 9:30 a.m.

"I *know*," Paula Williams assured her. "I've been here at the clinic for hours . . . Listen, they asked me to call you and tell you to come in."

"What?" Kathy put a hand up to her temple, shaking her head. "Look, I'm a little slow—haven't even had a coffee yet—but Matron Cassidy gave me the sack yesterday . . . Hasn't she told anyone?"

"I don't know. In any case, Roget wants you in here and as soon as possible."

"Paula, has something happened?"

There was silence.

"Paula?"

"Still here." She lowered her voice. "Yes, it *seems* as if something has happened all right. Just get in here fast, Kathy. Can't say any more. Have to go."

The line went dead and Kathy frowned at the instrument for a moment before hanging it up.

Brian still snored gently and hadn't moved off his back by the time Kathy threw on some clothes and hurried out.

Kathy could only think that it had something to do with Patrick. As she hurried through the drizzle towards the Roget Clinic, she saw a police car and an SEC truck outside the gates. Two men in overalls, wearing yellow hardhats and heavy rubber gloves were being raised towards the powerlines in a snorkel lift, the type that was called a "cherry picker."

There was also a knot of curious onlookers being kept away from the gates by two uniformed policemen. They stared coldly at her as she approached.

"My name is Katherine Jacquard. Doctor Roget sent for me."

"Go right in, Mrs. Jacquard," said the senior man, opening one of the gates for her.

She paused. "Can you tell me what has happened?"

"The Doctor and Detective Sergeant Grant are waiting for you. In Matron Cassidy's office, I believe." His tone and his face gave absolutely nothing away.

Grant was a big bullnecked, square-jawed man with short greying hair and the penetrating eyes that seemed to go with lawmen. He was sitting behind Matron's desk, toying with the jade dragon paperweight, and did not stand when Roget, who looked very agitated, introduced Kathy. He nodded curtly.

"Sit down, Mrs. Jacquard," he said and then set his bleak eyes on Roget again. "You were saying, Doctor?"

"I was saying," Roget replied frostily, "that I fail to see how a simple power blackout becomes a matter for the police. Surely, it's purely an SEC concern."

Kathy watched and listened bewilderedly, but intently.

"Well, it is not really as simple as all that," Grant said, boring his eyes into Roget. "We are talking about much more than a *simple* blown fuse."

"Well, I don't mean to play down the seriousness of what has happened," Roget answered with a nervous chuckle and a little wild look in Kathy's direction, "but it is all pretty well under control now, isn't it?"

Grant held his gaze for a moment, then looked at Kathy without change of expression before dropping his eyes to a notebook in front of him. He set down the paperweight.

"This Matron Cassidy has been contacted, I presume?"

"There was no reply from her home. I imagine she is on her way in to the clinic right now."

"Doctor—Sergeant," Kathy said. "Is there something here that involves me?"

Roget started to speak, but Grant cut him short.

"I'll be with you in a moment, Mrs. Jacquard . . . Now, Doctor, this Matron Cassidy phoned our office very recently for records on a patient here. Did you know?"

"Of course. I authorized it."

"Why?" Grant's mouth opened and closed like a bear trap.

"I like to know as much about my patients as possible." Roget flicked his eyes towards Kathy who was watching him silently.

"You are aware that certain allegations were made about this patient at the time of the accident? That there was certain evidence that pointed to him having electrocuted his own mother and her lover in a bath?"

Kathy put a hand to her mouth, covering a little gasp. It sounded very sinister the way Grant had said it.

"I gleaned as much from what records your department released," Roget said a little stiffly.

Grant regarded him steadily for a long moment, then swung his gaze to Kathy. "You were responsible for the patient in Room 15, daily, for the hours between noon and nine p.m., right?"

"Yes. But I should tell you that Matron Cassidy dismissed me yesterday."

Grant raised his eyebrows at Roget who shrugged.

Grant made a note. "We'll return to that. Now, Mrs. Jacquard, were you ever aware of anything unusual in Room 15?"

Kathy stiffened, felt some of the blood drain from her face. She tried to look unconcerned and to keep her voice level as she answered. "Sergeant, Patrick has been in a coma for three years. That in itself is unusual." She was very tense, feeling guilty.

"I daresay," Grant said dryly. "Anything else?"

124

Kathy looked bewildered. Roget was no help, just returning her enquiring look blankly. "I'm not sure what you mean. If you could be more specific, Sergeant . . . ?" *Did he know about last night?* she wondered. He picked up the dragon paperweight again and began to toy with it. "A Sister Panicale was found unconscious in Room 15 early this morning. In fact, more than unconscious . . ." He glanced at Roget for help.

"She was in a state of catatonic hysteria, Sister."

"Good God! What, what happened?" Kathy gasped.

"We had a power failure." Roget continued before Grant could speak this time, "My personal theory is that Panicale simply panicked. You know how she virtually existed on the edge of hysteria most of the time and was ill with a heavy cold. I think she tripped and struck her head, that is all."

He looked challengingly at Grant.

"It would explain the broken glass of the cabinet door, I suppose," the policeman admitted reluctantly.

"Is she going to be all right?" Kathy asked.

Roget made a "who knows?" gesture. "She is under heavy sedation. We can't get anything out of her."

"Which is why I thought *you* might be able to tell us something, Mrs. Jacquard," Grant said flatly. "But if you have not been here since yesterday you couldn't know what might have occurred last night."

Kathy shook her head, not trusting herself to speak, uneasy under Grant's steely gaze.

"Getting back to the power failure," the sergeant said abruptly. "The main power was off all over the neighbourhood, doctor. From about 9:30 p.m. till 10:27 p.m. Almost an hour. The SEC claims that the power overload originated here in your clinic."

"Well, it is entirely possible, I imagine," Roget said, plainly bewildered by all this. "Circuits *do* become overloaded in an establishment like this where power is being consumed constantly by machines that run twenty-four hours a day."

"You have got your own emergency generator, I suppose?"

"Of course. It cut in soon after the main power failure. It is an absolute necessity, Sergeant."

Grant nodded sourly; he didn't like the obvious being pointed out to him. He rustled his note papers irritably, lips moving silently as he read on. "The power failure occurred at 9:33 p.m. and we were swamped with calls from all over the neighbourhood. Not just to report the blackout, but everything from barking dogs to flying saucers, to some idiot claiming he was getting satellite coverage of World War II in his television set. In full colour! And all this began happening at 9:34 p.m. That is when we logged the first call. One minute exactly after the blackout started." He flicked his eyes from Roget to Kathy and back to Roget. "And the SEC reported enough of a power drain to run Luna Park for a week. Also, it seems at about the same time, this Sister Panicale experienced some sort of shock that put her into . . ." Grant broke off as the door opened after a perfunctory knock and a uniformed constable came hurrying in.

"There is something downstairs I think you should see," the constable said in a controlled voice.

Grant frowned at the young policeman, "Can't it wait?"

"No, it can't, sir," he replied.

Grant stood up and moved towards the door. "You two had better come with me," he said to Kathy and Roget.

Puzzled, they followed him out of Matron's office and into the lobby towards the stairs leading to the basement. A nurse was handing a grey-faced SEC worker a small glass of cloudy liquid which Kathy recognized as cloudy ammonia. He took it with shaking hands, downing it swiftly.

They didn't notice Matron Cassidy's shoes at the top of the stairs as they went down around the brick wall of the lift shaft. Kathy felt like she was choking, some premonition of something ghastly waiting down here made it difficult for her to breath. She almost bumped into Roget as he stopped suddenly when he rounded the last bend. Grant had hurried on ahead with the

126

constable. Kathy came down and stepped around Roget to see what had riveted him to the spot. Her knees quaked and her stomach knotted.

Over at the switchboard a bearded SEC worker stood, apparently unconcerned, talking with Grant and the white-faced constable. It was what was beside them that made Kathy gasp. Matron Cassidy's fried corpse —the side nearest Kathy reminding her of how Ed's hands had looked when the searing casserole pot had cooked the flesh off his bones—hung grotesquely from the main switch bars, her metal framed glasses welded to a mass of molten metal, supported by the chain around her neck. Molten copper had sprayed over her hair and embedded itself in her flesh. Most of her clothing had been reduced to blackened rags.

The stench was nauseating and Kathy put a handkerchief over her mouth.

Grant came back, putting out his arms, ushering Kathy and Roget back onto the stairs, around the first corner, out of sight of the corpse.

"There is the cause of your power failure," he said, breathing a little raggedly. "SEC man says she was standing in a puddle of water in stockinged feet, and must have touched the switch for some reason. The glasses' frame jumped up and short-circuited the terminals. The buzz-bars vaporized, molten copper sprayed everywhere . . ."

"I think we can imagine what happened quite well enough without your graphic description, Sergeant!" Kathy breathed.

Grant looked surprisingly contrite. "Yeah, sure. I'm sorry, Mrs. Jacquard." He turned to the stricken Roget. "Who was she?"

"Matron Cassidy."

Grant pursed his lips. "Now what would she be doing at the fuse-box? Especially when she was supposed to have left the building almost half an hour earlier?"

Roget shook his head dumbly.

Grant turned his quizzical gaze to Kathy but she, too, shook her head. The policeman sighed. "Well, you will want to have these switches checked out, of

127

course, but for the moment I'm prepared to call it an accident."

It had stopped raining when Kathy came out of the clinic and she folded her raincoat neatly over her arm as she stood on the porch. The door opened behind her and Sergeant Grant came out, nodding to her.

"I'll walk you to the gate," he said and took her elbow, urging her down the wet path. "You sure you don't know why Matron Cassidy gave you the sack?"

"I told you, Sergeant, she would not give me a reason. I could only surmise."

"That it had something to do with the patient in Room 15?"

"Yes. I am not prepared to say any more."

He stopped her and turned her to face him. "I am a policeman, Mrs. Jacquard. I have been trained to sense things, and I sense that you think there was more to Matron Cassidy's death than just an accident."

Kathy's teeth tugged at her lower lip and her hands mangled her raincoat.

"Do you know something I should know, Mrs. Jacquard?"

Kathy had already made other embarrassing attempts to have someone believe her about Patrick. People in the medical profession who should have at least admitted the possibility that she could have been partially right. But, to tell a hard-headed policeman who dealt only in cold facts and expect him to believe her . . . ?

"Patrick, the patient in Room 15, depends on a life-support system to keep him alive, Sergeant. Any interruption to the power supply could—probably would—kill him."

Grant considered her words for a long minute. "Are you saying Matron Cassidy was trying to kill this Patrick?"

"She had discussed euthanasia with me not long ago."

He shook his head. "She would know the emergency generator would cut in within a minute."

"It is down in the basement, too. She could have planned to switch it off as well." Kathy was breathing quickly now, tense again, her face strained under Grant's bleak gaze.

"Serious allegations, Mrs. Jacquard. You are sure it's not based on any bitterness you may feel towards Matron Cassidy for having fired you?"

Kathy flushed. "That is not what is behind my *allegations,* Sergeant, I can assure you!"

"Okay. Tell me what is behind them?"

Kathy licked her lips. "There, there is someone who could explain it better than I can. I . . . I think it might pay you to talk with him."

Grant studied her soberly. "Who, Mrs. Jacquard?"

Kathy hesitated, then said, with a rush, "Doctor Brian Wright. He's a neuro-surgeon at Southern General!"

Grant's eyes narrowed. "What could he tell me?"

"I'm not sure. But he is conversant with Patrick and what he is capable of. I think it's important that you talk with him, Sergeant. Please!"

Grant mulled it over and Kathy looked out into the street towards the sound of clanking, thinking it was the SEC crew at work. But, beyond the truck she saw a tow truck, a parking warden standing beside the operator as he hitched up the chains to the small Triumph sports car, preparing to tow it away from the "No Standing" zone.

"All right, Mrs. Jacquard. We will see this Doctor Wright."

Kathy didn't know whether to feel relieved or not. As she was getting into the police car, she glanced back towards the open window of Patrick's room.

Doctor Roget stood there, arms folded across his thin chest, staring at her with his bug eyes.

In the room behind him, Paula Williams brushed up the last of the broken glass from the floor and stood, wearily. Patrick lay in the bed, the EEG head harness removed. The monitors seemed to be registering lower than usual. Williams pointed it out to Roget as he turned away slowly from the window. He studied the dials and screens closely.

129

"Everything seems to be absolutely minimal, doctor," Williams said. "Is he all right?"

Roget straightened and looked down at Patrick, the large blue eyes staring up at ceiling. He put out a hand and rested it on his naked shoulder.

"No," he said very quietly. "He is not doing too well at all. Perhaps that power surge last night . . . I don't know . . . Something. I'm inclined to think that Patrick's time has come." He nodded in emphasis. "Yes, I really think his time has come."

Chapter Thirteen

They found Doctor Brian Wright in the grounds of
Southern General. He was with two colleagues, dressed
in white coat, with stethoscope in hand, and apparently deep in earnest conversation, when Kathy
called his name.

She saw him stiffen, pause, then continue talking
without turning his head. She called a second time,
aware of the bulky form of Grant beside her. This time
Brian gave a rather stiff smile to his colleagues and
then turned, waving to Kathy. The other two doctors
continued walking on, slowly. Brian came back towards
Kathy, casting a querying look at Grant.

Kathy introduced them, apologizing to Brian for
interrupting him and adding, "Matron Cassidy has been
electrocuted."

"Good God!" he breathed and she knew by his sharp
look that he immediately considered Patrick's involve-
ment. It encouraged her.

"Sergeant Grant is investigating. Sister Panicale was
found in Room 15, in a state of catatonic hysteria."
Kathy was tense and excited, and the words seemed
to fall over one another.

Brian frowned. "Wait a moment—Sister Panicale?"
He glanced at Grant as if for clarification, something
more straightforward than he was getting from Kathy.

"When Mrs. Jacquard says I am 'investigating,' Doctor," Grant told him, "it is pretty much routine from
what I can see. There was an electrical accident and

this other nurse fell in the darkness during the black-out. We had to look into it, of course."

Brian nodded, still obviously puzzled. "How do I come into it, Sergeant?" He was plainly hoping Kathy had not involved him.

"Matron Cassidy was trying to switch off the power when she was killed, Brian!" Kathy put it swiftly.

Brian frowned, looking blank, and Kathy had a terrible, cold, sinking feeling in her belly. She had noticed some reaction in him when she had introduced Grant as a policeman, but that had been understandable enough. Now . . .

"Patrick was right, don't you see, Brian?" Kathy said almost pleadingly, trying to will him to back her up. "He said someone would try to kill him last night and . . . and she did try. But he *stopped* her!"

Grant frowned. *"He* stopped her? You are not talking about the patient in the coma are you, Mrs. Jacquard?"

Kathy put a shaking hand to her temple. "I, I know it sounds crazy, Sergeant, that is why I brought you to see Doctor Wright, I thought he could explain better than I can . . ."

Her voice trailed off and there was an awkward silence. She hated Brian then for the blank look he had put on his face. Not only blank, but pitying.

"Well, I'm not, uh, sure just what is it you're after, Kathy." He gave Grant a helpless, "Don't-ask-me" kind of look and the policeman nodded very slightly; two men with an emotionally-distraught woman on their hands . . .

"Brian," she said desperately, making one more plea. "I, I know it's awkward for you, but Matron has been *killed!* We have to do . . . something!"

"I am really sorry, Kathy," Brian said innocently. "But how do you think I can help?"

"Tell him about psychokinesis, life-forces, the Kirlian aura. Oh, please, Brian. *Tell him!*"

Brian smiled faintly, "Kathy, I would be happy to give Sergeant Grant a four-hour lecture on psycho-kinesis or the other subjects you mentioned, but I hardly see that these things can have anything to do with Matron Cassidy's death."

"Nor can I," Grant said flatly, glancing pointedly at his watch.

Kathy raised her voice for the first time and Brian's waiting colleagues looked towards her sharply. "Damn it, if you don't say something, he will think I am a, a lunatic!"

Brian glanced at the other doctors, made a shrugging, apologetic motion and sighed heavily as he turned back to Grant and frowned deeply at Kathy. She was grasping at straws now.

"The swimming pool! Tell him about that night in the swimming pool, Brian!"

"You mean the night I got the cramp?"

"It *wasn't* cramp!" She made a frantic effort to keep the rising hysteria out of her voice. "It was *him! Patrick!*"

"Oh, for Christ's sake!" muttered Grant and Brian laughed derisively.

Suddenly, Kathy was very calm, very steady. It was useless trying to get Brian to back her up, she knew that. Her eyes narrowed and she shook off his hand as he put it on her arm.

"Kathy, love, I think . . ."

"Don't patronize me!" she said between her teeth, drilling her gaze into him coldly. "But I think it is time we told *Detective* Sergeant Grant about last night, don't you, Doctor Wright?"

Brian flushed, "I hardly think that is a police matter." He gave a nervous laugh.

"Shall I allow him to judge for himself?"

Grant had had enough. He saw the sparring between these two, put it down to a lovers' hassle and glanced at his watch again. As Kathy started to speak, he interrupted her. "Would you wait in the police car, please, Mrs. Jacquard?"

"No thank you, Sergeant, I . . ."

"I was being polite," he cut in coldly. "But now it is an order, Mrs. Jacquard: *wait in the car.*"

Kathy bristled but then her shoulders slumped as a

133

feeling of hopelessness hit her hard. She studied Brian for a few, incredibly-illuminating moments, then simply walked off, leaving him with Grant.

"All right, doctor," Grant said as she moved towards the police car at the gates. He had adopted a man-to-man tone. "Just what did happen last night?"

Brian gave him a sly smile. "You are not really interested in my sex life, are you, Sergeant?"

Grant grinned, nodding understandably. "Thought I detected a bit of a lovers' tiff there. Know her well?"

Brian shrugged. "I have dated her once or twice. She is recently separated from her husband. Going through a pretty rough time one way or another. I mean, this Patrick was obviously too much of a handful for her. She was depressed to start with and working with comatose patients is enough to lower anyone's spirits. She was alone with him for nine hours at a time. I think she was beginning to imagine he was conscious, or something. I know there was some conflict between her and Matron Cassidy, Doctor Roget, too, over her views." He laughed shortly. "At one stage, she apparently believed he was *controlling* people!"

"Pretty weird. She didn't seem too unstable until she brought me here, but I guess, as you say, it is all symptoms of her marriage break-up. She said Matron mentioned euthanasia. As long as there was a chance Matron Cassidy *might* have been trying something, I had to check."

Brian gave him a wide smile. "Don't worry about it, Sergeant, quite understandable." He glanced at his own watch and then towards the other two doctors who were growing impatient.

"Still," Grant said just as Brian started to make his excuses for leaving. "It was kind of strange, Matron mucking about at the switchboard in stockinged feet at that time of night. Don't you think?"

Brian was tense again now. "Well, I believe the patient, Patrick, is on life-support system. If Matron Cassidy had wanted to . . . let him die, all she had to do was switch it off for a while. There would hardly be any need to shut down the entire clinic."

"She blacked-out the whole bloody block!"

"Well, there you are. Talk about overkill!"

Grant studied him for a moment and then nodded, giving him a mirthless smile. "Guess you're right. Sorry to have troubled you, Doctor."

"Not at all, Sergeant. Glad to have been of help. Even if it was only in a negative sort of way!"

Brian waved casually and hurried across to where his colleagues waited.

Grant watched the three of them walk into the hospital building and then, lips pursed thoughtfully, started back to the police car. He could see Kathy's white face at the front passenger window.

Doctor Roget switched on the electroencephalograph machine and adjusted the headset on Patrick again. He pressed the electrodes against his scalp and temples, making sure there was good contact, then walked back to the graph paper, lowered the needles into position. He pressed the buttons that set the roller turning, feeding the paper through under the series of electronically-operated needles. Only straight lines showed.

There was no cerebral activity registering.

His expression rather grim, Roget went to the monitor dials and read them off. Respiration—minimal. Heart—minimal. Pulse—weak.

He decided to hook up the dialysis unit. Patrick was not scheduled for a blood exchange just now, but Roget felt it might make a difference. He was *almost* willing to allow him to die, to just fade away as he appeared to be doing now, but the scientist in him urged him to try every possible means to keep that mysterious "life-force" flickering, to prolong it just a little longer, perhaps re-activate it and give him more time to identify it.

By God, the name of Roget would ring throughout the Halls of Medical Science for all Eternity if he was successful.

He looked up quickly as the door of the room opened and Kathy Jacquard stood there. Roget straightened, his attitude stiff and cool.

135

"Have you forgotten that you no longer work here, Mrs. Jacquard?"

"I . . . I just came to say goodbye to Patrick," Kathy said haltingly. There was a strangeness about Roget which disturbed her.

"Have a nice chat with the police sergeant?"

Kathy ignored that, walked over to the bedside and looked down at Patrick, noticing how pale he was. There seemed to be dark circles under his eyes.

"He doesn't look as well as he did."

"I think he is dying." Roget sighed. "I suppose it is for the best."

"Best for whom, Doctor?"

His shoulders slumped. "Everyone. Him. Us. Matron knew it all along. I was the one who resisted. She had to die before I was convinced she was right. But I can't let him go without making some effort. I am supposed to *save* life!"

"Are you trying to convince yourself that you have acted, *are* acting, responsibly, Doctor?"

"I do not have to take that from you, Jacquard, whether you work here or not!" For a moment, he looked unbalanced.

"No, you don't." She gestured to Patrick. "He killed Matron. He killed her, just as surely as he is listening to us now."

Roget stared down at Patrick. He looked again at the dials and monitors and their low readings. Something suddenly snapped in him. His lower lip trembled, he nodded constantly.

"Horrible! Horrible!" he said, breathing harder. "We worked together for many years. Didn't always agree, in fact, seldom agreed. She died because we differed in our beliefs about him." He sighed heavily. "And I was about to betray her memory by . . ." Roget straightened slowly and looked steadily at Kathy. "He is like a cancer. He attaches himself to this building and starts to grow. And the more a cancer grows, the more it chokes the life out of everything around it, Mrs. Jacquard."

"He is no different to the rest of us, Doctor. He is alone and scared."

"No, no, you are mistaken. A cancer can't be scared. It doesn't have feelings, can't be aware. It just consumes and destroys." He turned his gaze on Patrick. "No one is sad when a cancer dies." A cold smile flicked on and off.

"Well, I am not so sure that he is dying, doctor." Kathy said slowly. "He looks exhausted. I think he is only resting."

Roget shook his head slowly. "Oh, no. He's dying. I can assure you of that, Jacquard." He smiled wider, a strange smile. A promise? Kathy frowned slightly, not exactly sure of what Roget was saying. But she shook herself. It was this damn room again, influencing her mood, she had come to say goodbye and that was just what she intended to do. She reached down and laid a hand gently on Patrick's forehead, just below the EEG harness.

"Goodbye, Patrick," she said quietly. "I am sorry I couldn't help you. But I tried." As she lifted her gaze to Roget she thought the needles on the monitor dials flickered across but it was so fast she could not be sure. "I'll say goodbye to you too, Doctor Roget."

"Farewell, Jacquard. Farewell." He sounded distant, his mind on other things.

Kathy left the room and looked into Room 17 where Captain Fraser was seated on the edge of his bed, slouch hat jammed on the back of his head, staring out the window.

"I'm leaving, Captain. I have come to say goodbye," Kathy said quietly.

He turned his head slowly, looked her up and down, then grinned. "Hit our communications last night, they did. Very smart, the Hun. Put us out of action for a while. Waitin' for the casualty list now. Be a lot more before this push is over, mark my words."

Kathy squeezed his thin shoulder, smiling faintly. "Goodbye, Captain."

He didn't watch her go, but returned to gazing out

of the window. Kathy found Williams and they walked towards the main doors of the clinic side by side.

"What are you going to do?" Paula asked.

Kathy paused at the foot of the stairs, frowning thoughtfully. She looked back and upwards. "I feel as if there is something more for me to do here, but of course that's out of the question."

"Look, the best thing you can do is go out that door and close it very firmly behind you. Whatever Patrick is, he is no good for you."

Kathy glanced at Paula's face and sighed heavily. Then she smiled faintly. "You know, Paula, I think I might find Ed and ask him if he wants to—play house."

"Good idea. All the luck in the world. Keep in touch."

"Sure," Kathy smiled and squeezed Williams' arm as she hurried towards the main doors, eager to see what Ed would have to say to her suggestion.

Williams watched her go rather sadly now and, her mind on Kathy and their friendship, she unthinkingly walked over to the lift doors with their "Out of Order" sign and pushed the button. It was several moments before she realized what she had done and she stepped back, glancing up at the indicator. It showed that the lift was still jammed between the top and first floors. Giving herself a mental dig in the ribs to wake up, Paula Williams hurried towards the stairs and began to climb them.

As she did so, there was a distinct clattering sound from the lift shaft, like someone dropping a heavy tool.

But Williams did not hear.

Chapter Fourteen

Kathy still had her front door key to the house she had shared with Ed and she used it quietly, slipping inside and closing the door gently behind her.

Even as she called out "Surprise, surprise!" she smelled the musty odour, a staleness in the air that a house gets when it is closed up for a time. She frowned when there was no answer and walked into the living room. Ashtrays overflowed with stale cigarette butts, empty beer cans were on the floor beside the easy chairs, a newspaper was draped over the television set, one of Ed's jackets and a soiled denim shirt hung from the handle of a cupboard door.

Kathy moved to the other rooms. The kitchen sink was filled with dirty dishes and cups. The bathroom had socks and underpants hanging from the shower rail, hastily and improperly washed. In the bedroom, the bed had not been made and the sheets needed laundering. The washing machine was stuffed with clothes that had been washed but never taken out.

In the garage, she found Ed's car, keys in the ignition.

Worried, Kathy went back into the house and sat down in the chair near the television. She glanced at the date on the newspaper. Two days old. It looked as if Ed had not been home for two days. But why? she wondered. Where could he be? He had heavily-bandaged hands but he wouldn't go anywhere without taking his car. The bandages wouldn't stop him driving. There was something queer here.

Her heart lurched as, for a moment, the thought of Patrick flashed into her mind. What was it she—he—had typed? "Now Ed's the one all boxed-in and hung-up . . ." But that didn't make any sense.

She jumped as the phone suddenly rang and she ran to it, snatching up the receiver, hoping it was Ed.

"Yes . . . ?" Kathy stiffened. "Brian! How did you get this number?"

"Looked it up in the book when I couldn't get any reply at your flat," Brian told her easily, with a forced brightness. "Kathy, I want to apologize for this morning."

"All right, Brian," Kathy said without expression.

"Jesus, Kathy! I mean, you threw me for a loop bringing a cop around that way . . . What did you expect from me?"

Kathy sighed, feeling curiously "dead" as she listened to Brian. "Nothing, Brian. I did not, and do not, expect anything from you. Thanks for ringing."

"No, wait! Don't hang-up! Don't end things this way, Kath! Do you have any idea at all what would happen to my career if they found out that we, I . . ."

"Just forget it, Brian," she cut in dully. "Forget the whole damn thing. It simply does not matter any more. Nothing does!"

"Not even last night?" he asked, with a brief laugh.

Kathy sighed. "Does it matter to you?"

"Hell, yes! It was terrific!"

"Fine. Terrific for you. So-so for me. You are not the great lover you think you are, Brian. You are not the great—anything. Good-bye." She crashed the phone onto the rest and stood behind it, mouth pulled into a tight line. As she looked around at the familiar walls, the framed prints she and Ed had selected and hung in happier days, she began to feel guilty about last night and a lot of other things. She sat down, opened the Teledex and selected a number against the name "Phil." She dialled swiftly.

"Phil, Kathy Jacquard . . . Yes, it has been a long time. Well, I would ask Ed if I knew where he was . . . That is why I'm ringing, thought you might . . . Oh, a

140

couple of days . . . He had this accident, burnt his hands at my flat . . ." She forced a laugh. "No! Not on me! . . ." She sobered. "Thanks, Phil . . . I'll try the pub, then."

She hung up and dialled the number he had given her but the barman said that Ed was not in and had not been for a couple of days.

"Tell you what, though, Mrs. Jacquard," the man added. "He was talking about buying a car . . ."

"A car?" Kathy asked blankly, thinking of the Chrysler in the garage. "You mean he was going to get rid of the Chrysler . . . ?"

"No, I don't think so. He was after a particular kind of car. Sports job. A Triumph, he said. Something he reckoned he should have bought years ago . . ."

Kathy frowned, a memory stirring of a tow truck outside the clinic taking away a small Triumph sportscar that had been parked in the "No Standing" zone. She shook her head, came back to the present. "I beg your pardon? I didn't hear . . ."

"I told him about a bloke I knew who had one for sale," the barman repeated. "Fellow named Neil Adler. He's out of work, does a few odd jobs around the pub and he was looking for a few extra bucks. I sent Ed around. I can give you Neil's number if you like . . . ?"

"I'd appreciate it very much," Kathy said and wrote swiftly. She thanked the barman again, hung up and then dialled Neil Adler's number.

He told her that Ed had bought the car from him and, though he sounded puzzled, he gave her the registration number. Kathy was shaking a little as she hung up. There was an idea, a *fear*, beginning to take shape in the back of her mind. It did not have form yet, because, subconsciously, she did not want to *really* think about it. Her breathing was a little faster, irregular.

Her hand shook as she picked up the phone book and looked up a number. Still she hesitated before dialling, holding the receiver in her hand, listening to the buzz of the open line. Then, with determination, she dialled and when a voice answered at the other end she swallowed and said,

"I would like to talk to Detective-Sergeant Grant in the CIB section . . . No, he won't know my name." She waited, teeth tugging at her bottom lip. "Oh, Sergeant Grant. This is Mrs. Jacquard. I, I was afraid you might not want to speak with me . . ."

"And why did you think that, Mrs. Jacquard?" Grant asked, sounding a little weary.

"Well, I made quite a fool of myself earlier—with Doctor Brian Wright . . ."

"That's all right, Mrs. Jacquard. I understand you were trying to help. Now, have you got some further information?"

"Oh, no, Sergeant. At least . . . Well, actually I wanted to ask you a favour."

There was a silence, only the vacuum-like hum of the line in her ear. "Sergeant?"

"What is the favour, Mrs. Jacquard?" Grant asked, with a slight edge in his voice. Clearly, whatever it was, he would rather not get involved.

"Well, it's my husband, Ed," she began. Aware that he must be impatiently tapping his fingers on his desk at the other end of the line, she swiftly told him about Ed's accident and finding the house looking as if it had not been lived in for a couple of days.

"Maybe he has gone off somewhere," Grant suggested. "I know if I had a month off work, on a doctor's certificate, I would be off fishing."

"His car is here in the garage, Sergeant!" she said. "But I have managed to find out that he bought a Triumph sports car from a man named Neil Adler—and, well, that was one of the things we argued about so much: my wanting such a little car and Ed insisting we couldn't afford it. He wouldn't even let me go out to work to pay for it and . . ."

"Mrs. Jacquard," Grant broke in. "I have got a hell of a lot on my plate right now and . . ."

"I'm sorry, Sergeant. The point I was trying to make is that I am sure Ed bought that car for me. We were, well, I think we were on the way to a reconciliation and I think he bought the car as a kind of peace offering." She heard him make impatient sounds again and went

142

on swiftly. "There was such a car towed away from outside the clinic this morning when you and I were getting into your car. I remembered seeing it there for the last couple of days—in a 'No Standing' zone. Anyway, I was wondering if you could find out where it has been taken and see if the registration number checks. It's BTK-473 . . ."

Grant sighed. "Mrs. Jacquard, the Traffic Department handles those things. I'm CIB."

"Yes, but surely you know someone . . . ? Please, Sergeant. It is very important to me."

"Well, I can't see how it will you help you find your husband . . ."

Kathy put a smile in her voice. "Thank you, Sergeant. Will it take long?"

She could imagine Grant rolling his eyes ceilingwards. "I don't know. Might be some time. Better give me your number . . ."

Kathy did so and thanked him again, then hung up. She sat back in the chair beside the telephone table, chewing at her bottom lip again. She felt happy in one way, happy that Ed had bought her the car, for it meant there was a real chance they were getting back together.

But she was worried, too. Because, if it *had* been the car that had been towed away from outside the clinic, why hadn't Ed at least phoned to tell her it was waiting outside for her?

It was almost two days since she had first vaguely noticed the car parked there. Where on earth could Ed have gone? What could have happened to him?

The ugly black thought at the back of her mind began to nudge its way forward, relentlessly. Its name was Patrick.

Doctor Roget was beaten. He was forced to admit it after there was absolutely no change at all on the monitors at the end of the dialysis session. *Patrick* had beaten him.

He stood back in the room, staring at the monitor screens, as if willing them to increase their "minimal" readings, then swivelled his gaze to Patrick. Roget no longer looked quite sane.

"So, you are going to take your secret with you, eh?" he whispered. "You will not divulge it to me, you will not allow me to ride to fame and possibly fortune on your shoulders? Well, perhaps this is understandable. Our relationship has not been exactly amicable, has it? But I'm afraid you have had your last chance. To put it crudely, I've shot my bolt." He laughed quietly. "Now it is your turn."

He spun about as the door opened and Paula Williams came in.

"What do you want?" he snapped.

"Oh, Doctor, I'm on duty here. There is no one else available now that Kath, Mrs. Jacquard, has gone and Sister Panicale is under sedation . . ."

Roget smiled suddenly, walked towards Williams and took her elbow, turning her towards the door. "Don't worry about it, Sister. I'll take care of Patrick. Personally. I'll be working with him for quite some time yet. Why don't you just go home?"

Williams blinked, glancing at her watch instinctively. "Home?"

"Yes," Roget smiled and the strange look on his face frightened Williams a little. He urged her to the door. "Take the afternoon off. We can manage quite well."

He laughed again and Williams gave him a weak, fleeting smile, glancing briefly at the immobile Patrick. "Well, Doctor, if you are sure . . ."

"Yes, yes, I'm sure. Home you go. Have a good time." Roget practically pushed her out into the corridor, closed the door and leaned back against it, the smile gone from his face now. He stared at Patrick, straightened and turned the door handle again. "Don't go away, Patrick. I will be right back. Right back!"

As the door closed behind him, the needles on the dials began to rise slowly but powerfully.

Ed Jacquard was dying.

His breath rasped in the back of his throat as he tried to breathe the thick, noxious air of the lift that

144

had been his prison for over thirty-six hours. It had stopped between floors just after he had stepped into it with the bouquet of flowers for Kathy, with the car keys in the small envelope attached to the stems with a blue ribbon.

Now they lay withered and mashed on the filthy floor of the lift. The steel box stank. His throat was painfully dry. All body moisture seemed to have been long used up in his frantic efforts to break out of his prison. Beard stubble rasped on his face and jaw.

He had not been idle. The bandages hung from his mangled hands in trailing rags, spotted with fresh and dried blood. There was a domed series of dents in the ceiling where he had been smashing at it with the metal grip bar he had finally managed to wrench from the wall after almost a day of straining. Every muscle in his body ached and throbbed. His head was thick and muzzy with fatigue as well as the lack of fresh air.

On his stomach now, he crawled across the floor to the doors and placed his nose and mouth close to the crack where they came together at floor level. There was the faintest zephyr of air filtering in and he dragged down what he could in noisy, screeching gulps. He knew it was not going to be enough to sustain him. His guts heaved and growled, twisted and convulsed with hunger and nausea. There was a tingling numbness in his arms.

While he had his face pressed against the crack in the doors, he tried to call out: "He-eeeee-lp!" He knew the word well enough—he had been screeching and bawling it for the thirty-six hours he had been trapped in here—but now it came out only as a bleat. His throat was too dry, vocal chords strained. But he tried again and this time he managed to register a deeper tone, but he simply did not have enough air to get out a really commanding bellow. Even at the beginning no one had heard him. The steel box was almost soundproof, an effective prison.

He clutched at the floor in sudden terror.

The lift slipped about a foot and jerked to a halt, the

145

floor seemed to come up and smash into his exhausted body.

"Jesus Christ!" he wheezed, glancing at the control box that he had smashed open in an effort to get at the wiring.

It would be ironic if he had damaged the circuits to the point where they would not hold the weight of the lift any longer. But somehow he no longer cared.

Death would be welcome, he thought woozily.

Doctor Roget stood in his laboratory, staring at his frogs as they crawled over one another and flattened their bodies against the glass. He seemed deep in thought about something and slowly his gaze moved from the glass case to the desiccator jar further along the bench, the one he had used as a lethal gas chamber to exterminate the frogs before he had experimented on them.

In the bottom chamber was the pale cyanide solution that he had neglected to flush down the drain.

Roget smiled as he moved around the bench to a glass-fronted cabinet on the wall, opened it and brought out a heavy hypodermic syringe. He whistled softly as he walked back to the desiccator, removed the lid and then took out the ventilated partition that covered the lower chamber.

He placed the needle deep into the pale liquid and slowly pulled back the plunger. The cyanide solution swirled into the graduated cylindrical chamber.

"Much, *much* more certain than merely switching off the power supply," Roget murmured.

When the cylindrical syringe was full, Roget wiped the needle on a piece of cotton wool and holding it over the sharp steel carefully placed the hypodermic in the pocket of his white coat and went out the door.

Behind him, the frogs thumped against the glass walls of their prison, croaking. But no one heard the muffled sounds.

"Jesus Christ," he wheezed, glancing at the control

Chapter Fifteen

When the phone rang, Kathy fairly leapt across the
room and snatched it up off the rest.

"Yes?" she said breathlessly.

"Grant," the Sergeant's rough voice barked in her
ear. "You all right, Mrs. Jacquard?"

"Oh, yes, Sergeant. I, uh, just ran to answer the
phone, that's all. Were you able to check the car number for me?"

"Yes. It is the same one all right."

Kathy sucked down a sharp breath. "Then that
means Ed left it outside the clinic two days ago and
he hasn't been seen since!"

"You're sure? I mean, there were no keys in the
car. It was locked up tight. He didn't leave the keys
for you, maybe with a note, at the hospital reception
desk?"

Kathy frowned, "I don't know. I didn't check."

"Well, maybe you had better give them a ring. From
what I gather you had a pretty rough time with this
Patrick character, Mrs. Jacquard."

Kathy was startled by the sudden switch of subject.
She was anxious to check with the hospital desk. Ed
could have left the keys to the car there and with a
message for her.

"A comatose patient is not as easy to care for as
many people think, Sergeant," she said neutrally. "But
now if I . . ."

"Doctor Roget asked for his file from this office. It
has been returned now and landed on my desk, because

147

of the business with that nurse in Room 15." Kathy was listening intently now. She guessed that by "returned," Grant meant he had taken it back from Roget. "You don't strike me as the hysterical type, Mrs. Jacquard, and the way you traced your husband to that car was a good bit of detecting." A sour note entered his voice. "Wish some of my men showed as much nouse. Anyway, I read through Patrick's file. He is a bit of a celebrity, in our book anyway."

Kathy gripped the phone tightly now. "How do you mean?"

"Well, it is pretty certain he murdered his mother and her lover in that bath, but it didn't stop there. Been a number of queer things since." She heard pages turning as he checked a file or note book. "Someone has pencilled in a notation about the boyfriend of a nurse who worked with Patrick about a year ago. He died of some unspecified and exotic disease . . . Seems he lost all sensation in his limbs, starting in his hands. He could belt his fingers with a hammer and not feel it. But he did complain about tingling or numbness gradually creeping up his arms before he died . . ."

Kathy was very tense now, twisting the phone wire around her hand. She was remembering how Ed had not felt the pain of those severe burns.

"Seems another nurse was found unconscious in his room, too," Grant continued. "At Lochart. She had a complete breakdown . . ."

"Sergeant," Kathy broke in. "Thank you for telling me these things and for all you have done. But I really do have to go now. Goodbye."

Kathy pressed down the phone rest, breaking the connection. She let it rise again and when there came the buzz of the open line, she dialled the Roget Clinic's number swiftly . . .

The switchboard in the Roget Clinic lobby buzzed with the incoming call and the desk nurse glanced towards the flashing light, but hesitated. She looked back to Paula Williams, now in her street clothes, and to Roget who stood at the desk, in his white coat, hands thrust deep into his pockets, a strange smile on his face.

"I mean it, Nurse," he said to the desk nurse. "You can sign off, too, just like Sister Williams, and go home."

"But, Doctor," the nurse began, feeling a little bewildered, glancing again at the buzzing switchboard. "Excuse me while I answer that, Doctor . . ."

"Leave it!" he snapped and she jumped, spinning back towards him at his command. He forced his odd smile again. "I can do that. You just get your things and go on home."

Paula Williams straightened. "Look, Doctor Roget, we are already short-handed and . . ."

"I still own this clinic," Roget cut in curtly. "I know what I am doing. Go on home, both of you!"

The nurse looked to Williams for a lead and Paula shrugged helplessly, picked up her handbag and moved towards the door. The desk nurse did not like being left alone with Roget in this strange mood, so she muttered her thanks and swiftly ducked out from behind the desk. The switchboard continued to buzz. She hesitated again, casting a uneasy glance towards it. Roget widened his fixed smile and went around behind the desk, waving her away with his left hand. His right hand fondled the hypodermic syringe in his pocket. He breathed a sigh of relief as the nurse finally moved away down the corridor and Williams went out the front door. It had taken long enough to get rid of those two. Now the nurse was looking back to see if he was answering the incoming call, blast it.

He knew well enough how to operate the switch. He plugged in the cord, picked up the receiver. "Yes?" he snapped.

At the other end of the phone, Kathy had been about to hang up. Now she snatched back the receiver. "Hello? Hello? . . . Roget Clinic? . . . I want to speak with the desk, please . . . Who is that?"

"There is no one here," Roget said curtly, gruffly. "I'm the . . . janitor. You will have to ring back."

He hung up swiftly, pulled out the cords that were

149

already connected and switched off the power. Then, covertly looking at the syringe in his pocket, making sure it had not leaked unduly, he came out from behind the desk and began climbing the stairs slowly, trying to remember where the other staff on duty were. They would all thank him for giving them an unexpected holiday, he thought . . .

Sergeant Grant sounded slightly exasperated when he answered his phone and Kathy spoke to him again. He made no attempt to cover the sigh he gave.

"Yes, what is it *now,* Mrs. Jacquard?"

Kathy sounded agitated. "Sergeant, I'm sorry to trouble you again, but there is something badly wrong at the Roget Clinic!"

"Aw, hell, Mrs. Jacquard, I was just begining to think Doctor Wright had been mistaken about you—now you are proving me wrong! We have been over all this, haven't we? I mean, I admit the file on this Patrick person makes very strange reading, but, at the same time . . . "

"I just called the clinic," Kathy cut in, sounding a little desperate now. "To see if Ed had left the keys to the Triumph at the desk . . . A man answered and said there was no one there, that I should call back. He said he was the janitor . . ."

"Doesn't sound like anything is wrong, so far," Grant said. "Normal enough, isn't it? The desk nurse was obviously off some place and . . ."

"It was Roget himself!" Kathy blurted out. "I know his voice. It was Doctor Roget."

There was a short silence. "You are absolutely certain?" Grant asked quietly.

"Yes! Absolutely, Sergeant!"

"Hmmm . . . Any idea why he would be answering the switch and claiming to be the janitor?"

"None at all. But he sounded strange. In fact, he was acting very strange when I left the clinic. He was in Room 15 with Patrick. I told him I thought Patrick's monitors were so low because I, I felt he was just resting, recuperating if you like. But Roget said, no, he was dying. *Definitely* dying. When he said that, well, I'm sure all the needles flicked right across the dials, but it was too fast to be absolutely certain. You see, Sergeant, it was the *way* Roget spoke. As if he might finish the job Matron Cassidy started! And I am sure Patrick has done something to my husband . . ."

"Now, hold on, hold on! Let's not get too carried away," Grant said. "I agree there could be cause to look into things a little closer . . ."

"Will you meet me at the clinic right away?" Kathy asked, pleading. "Please, Sergeant! I am sure it's urgent."

"Well, look I'll have to . . ."

"I'm sorry, Sergeant. I can't spend any more time talking. I have got to get out there! Ed is in danger, I know it!" She hung up and snatched her handbag as she dashed across the room, thankful that Ed's car was in the garage with the keys in the ignition . . .

Grant frowned at the dead phone in his hand, lips pursed thoughtfully. Then he looked up the clinic number in his notebook and dialled.

There was only a constant screech on the line. The number did not connect, which mean it was out of order. It was enough for Grant. He had better get out there before that damn woman did something stupid.

Roget relaxed as he stepped into Room 15 and leaned back against the door. He had sent the staff home, one by one, as he had found them. Now there were only the patients and himself. And he was only interested in *one* patient.

Patrick.

The monitors showed minimal response. Roget moved to the bedside and stared down at Patrick. He frowned a little. There had been no change of expression, of course, but he would swear that Patrick looked more—alert? Impossible, he thought, and carefully withdrew the syringe from his pocket. He removed the wrapping of cotton wool from around the needle, held the hypodermic up and pressed the plunger a little to force out the bubble of air left by leakage.

151

It was an instinctive action, one he had performed thousands of times over the years, removing all the air from the cylinder before administering an injection. Then he laughed shortly, remembering *what* he was going to inject. In the light of that, an air bubble could hardly do much harm! He chuckled quietly and felt the breeze coming through the open window on his face as he leaned down, reaching for Patrick's arm with his left hand.

The EEG head harness was still in position and Roget lowered the needle towards the pinched-up skin of Patrick's bicep. He froze.

There was a faint click and a hissing sound. He spun swiftly. The graph paper moved very slowly out of the EEG unit. The electronic needles kicked violently, registering a massive peak of brain activity.

Roget turned his head to stare down at Patrick. As he did so he heard a distant clank and a thump. He thought, vaguely, that the sound at the edge of his consciousness was like the lift motor kicking over but failing to start. Then he slowly withdrew the needle from near Patrick's arm, watching the frantic needles on the EEG. They dropped back to their stable positions and the paper showed only straight lines— minimal activity.

Intrigued now, Roget pinched up the flesh on Patrick's arm again and waited. Nothing happened. Still minimal activity. But when he moved the needle closer to the flesh, the paper rolled out, the needles jerked almost off the paper and, distantly, there was that clanking thump again. He was sure now that it came from the lift shaft and briefly wondered why it should occur each time the EEG unit cut in. It was a machine that took very little power to operate . . .

He stopped that line of thought. There was something else here of much more importance.

"Patrick," Roget breathed. "I do believe that Jacquard woman may not have imagined everything she claimed had happened after all! You *have* been hiding your light under a bushel, haven't you? You are indeed aware!" Perspiration trickled down Roget's face. "But it is no good now. You are a cancer and you must be destroyed!"

He looked quickly towards the window-ledge as he heard a rattling sound. The potted plant, the cyclamen, was quivering, vibrating. He frowned, then turned back to Patrick, knowing what he had to do, prepared to take full responsibility.

It was something that should have been done long ago. He could not allow anything to stop him now.

In one swift motion, Roget grabbed Patrick's arm, pinched up the flesh and stabbed the needle towards it, thumb ready to ram the plunger home and send the lethal cyanide solution squirting into the bloodstream.

The potplant hurtled across the room as if shot from a cannon and struck Roget on the side of the head.

He reeled, slammed violently into the wall, and fell to the floor, the hypodermic rolling half under the bed. Roget sprawled there, blood on his temple, the pot shattered at his feet, soil mixture and the cyclamen plant resting on one of his shoes.

Graph paper rolled out of the EEG, the needles registering increased and powerful cerebral activity.

Ed Jacquard would have screamed if he had enough air in his lungs. His fingers seemed to dig into the floor of the lift.

There had been two or three metallic clanks from the shaft high above his head and each time the lift had jerked, falling slightly. He had been jarred out of his lethargy and, despite himself, his brain had started ticking over in his head which still felt stuffed with knotted string.

The Roget Clinic had been built about seventy years ago, he reckoned. It had a basement, ground floor and two floors above, all served by the lift. Being in the building game Ed knew that when the old mansion was constructed, as an elegant colonial home for some rich member of Melbourne's society, each floor would have been from four to five metres. Allowing another four metres for the basement and the fact that the lift was jammed between the top two floors, he had close to sixteen metres below him. Sixteen metres straight down to solid rock-bottom . . .

It was enough to make him sit up, gasping and croaking for air, chest heaving.

He sat there, his back against the steel doors, wondering where he was going to find the energy to renew his assault on the roof. He had to get some air in here. Once he could fill his lungs with fresh air, he would have plenty of energy, and then he could smash a way out, climb onto the roof and then up the lift shaft— hopefully, before the lift fell the rest of the way down.

He looked at his hands. They were stiff and bloody and split, too weak to hold the bar he had been using. His chest heaved violently and searing pain knifed through him, his throat ached and he clawed at it as his mouth opened and he gasped raggedly.

Who the hell was he kidding? He couldn't even stand, let alone make another attempt to get free. His eyelids were heavy and a lot of white was showing as his eyeballs rolled up into his head.

The motor clanked and the lift jerked as it slipped another fifteen centimetres.

Ed gave a little moan but there was no other sign of life from him.

Doctor Roget put a hand to his temple, dazed. He jerked open his eyes as his fingers touched something wet and sticky. He stared down at the blood on his fingertips.

Then he came out of it swiftly, realizing what had happened and where he was.

He thrust himself to his feet, clawed at the wall as his legs seemed to turn to rubber. He lurched upright, glaring wildly at Patrick. The EEG machine was still rolling out the graph paper and the needles were jerking.

Roget made a animal sound way back in his throat, looked around, and snatched up a chair. The drip-feed bottles rattled violently on their stainless steel stand near the window. Roget raised the chair above his

154

head. He was suddenly slammed back violently against the wall, the breath gusting out of his thin body.

Grunting, Roget lurched off the wall, got his balance and, nearly hysterical, flung the chair at Patrick. He missed and the chair struck the stainless steel stand. The bottles smashed and the stand fell over with a metallic clatter against the window ledge, the top part jutting out about a third of a metre.

Roget was half bent over in his follow-through from flinging the chair, and now he suddenly straightened with a violent movement, lifting right up onto his toes. His arms and legs flew out, as if he was on one of those carnival rides where centrifugal force pins people to the walls as they spin around.

At the same time, the door jerked open and Roget was hurled back, through the doorway, to crash against the opposite wall across the passage. His whole frame shook, the back of his head smashed against the plaster with stunning force. His long legs buckled beneath him and he spilled into an untidy head in the passage, blood from the wound in his temple trickling down his cheek and dripping from his jawbone.

The door to Room 15 slammed shut solidly.

Chapter Sixteen

Kathy had always hated the traffic along Toorak Road. It was never-ending, day and night, constant streams of cars, trucks and trams. Once the trams stopped running for the night it was easier, but there was always a heavy stream of vehicles using the road.

Now, in the late afternoon, although it was not yet full peak-hour, the road seemed jammed tight. Waiting in line, Kathy could not help but think about the Triumph that had been towed away from outside the clinic. It was not that she cared about the car so much, it was the fact that Ed had cared enough about her to buy it for her.

Oh, God! she thought, making it a prayer. Why doesn't the traffic move? She was frightened for Ed. Patrick had done something to him, she knew it, but there was a possibility that he could already be dead.

She shuddered, gripping the steering wheel tightly. What kind of thing *was* Patrick? Where did he get this power to influence people, control inanimate objects? How? How could it be? This was no Hollywood movie with special effects and trick photography. She had *seen* what Patrick could do, hadn't had enough intelligence to realize that it was probably a small portion of his capabilities. Although, at the time, it hadn't seemed as if he had a lot in reserve . . . still, if his strength *had* been building all this time, what was it he had been feeding on? What was the driving force behind his powers? Certainly something more than glucose drips.

When the traffic jam occurred, the driver of the car beside Kathy had switched off his motor. Now, with the lines ahead beginning to move forward, the man hit the starter again. The motor turned over with a growl stuttered, missed firing, and as the man kept the contact, gradually ground to a stop. Flat battery, Kathy thought, easing the Chrysler forward. She hoped the driver didn't have to get anywhere in a hurry. Horns blasted. Then a coldness went through her. Electricity! God in Heaven, was it possible that Patrick's strength was reinforced by electricity? Because, if it was, they had been feeding him all this time, keeping him hooked up to so many electrically-powered machines . . .

And the massive power drain from the city's grid last night! What was it Grant had said: "Enough to run Luna Park for a week!"

Kathy felt utterly sick as the traffic line ground to a stop again . . .

Roget came around slowly, his head throbbing violently, his back sore, pelvis aching. He put up a shaking hand to the back of his head and winced, opened his eyes and started as he stared up at a wild apparition, a Demon!

It was a bat-like creature, with voluminous wings hanging from slopping shoulders, a head with pointed ears that jutted straight out from the side of the skull, and there was some sort of claw that prodded him. The stench was powerful and sickening. It screeched.

Heart thudding, Roget sat upright and felt faint with relief as he recognized Captain Fraser, seeing a clearer image now that he wasn't looking up from the floor at the old man silhouetted against the corridor ceiling lights. The Captain lowered his four-pronged walking aid and cackled again as Roget got to all fours, still shaking.

"Told yez it'd be on!" the Captain croaked. "Din I? Told yez the Hun was makin' a push!" He lifted the walking aid and jabbed it towards the door of Room 15. "An' I told yez he was one of 'em, din' I?" he

157

cackled again. "Serves yer right for not listenin' to me. Serves yer right!"

He turned and shuffled back to Room 17, his walking-aid *tap-dragging* in time with his head as he shook it. He gave Roget a final told-you-so look, then went into his room and closed the door after him.

Hair hanging wildly across his high forehead, Roger thrust to his feet, steadying himself against the wall. Blood dripped from his chin but he ignored it as he glared at the door of Patrick's room, remembering.

He lurched across the passage, grabbing the door handle and turning it, driving his body forward. Roget grunted as he walked into a solid, unmoving wall. The door did not even rattle in its frame. It was as if it was part of the main shell of the old building. Fumbling, he brought out a ring of keys on the end of a chain. He muttered to himself as he sought frantically amongst them, isolating the master key and inserting it into the lock.

He bared his teeth, turning the key with one hand, the door knob with the other. He pushed. Nothing moved. He shoved harder, twisting the key first one way then the other. He kicked at the base of the door, then stood back and hammered on it with his fists.

"Open this door, damn you!" he shouted, his voice cracking a little. "Do you hear me? I am in control here! Not you!"

But the door was immovable.

Roget stepped back, sagging against the opposite wall, panting, his clothes soaked with sweat now. His hands shook as he held them in front of his face. Then he slowly looked at the door and the green number on the woodwork—15. He frowned, the creases deepening gradually, as if he were concentrating on something. His head turned a little to one side, in a listening attitude.

He seemed very intent, his eyes focused on the numerals—1 and 5.

Then, somewhat dazed, he gave a slight nod, as if answering some question or command that only he could hear, and stood up straight, turning towards the

158

far end of the corridor. Roget started to walk forward, robot-like, the pupils of his eyes wide, apparently out-of-focus, as he made for the head of the stairs that led to the floor below.

Roget marched down them stiffly, one hand sliding down the rail. He came to the next floor, walked on across the landing, and started down the next flight to the ground floor. In the deserted lobby, Doctor Roget stood for a moment, looking around him with that dazed expression. He nodded slightly once again, answering some silent command, and turned down the passage that went beyond the wall sign that read: "Medical Staff Only."

His footsteps echoed hollowly from the deserted corridor—a measured, rhythmic tread, absolutely unlike his normal, catlike movements. He came to the door of his own laboratory and pushed it open, going inside to the familiar smells and sights of the equipment. He walked, apparently unseeing and uncaring, into a low bench and knocked over several stands that carried clamped glass funnels and pipettes. They crashed on top of a Liebig condenser and it shattered loudly. Racks of test tubes fell to the floor and the glass crunched under his boots as he continued across the long room to the rear corner where he kept the glass case of frogs.

There were three left, spotted, obscene, clambering up the transparent walls. One leapt at the clamped lid but fell back on top of his companions. They seemed agitated as Roget approached with a peculiar expression on his face. He picked up the whole glass case and turned, knocking over piles of notes and expensive equipment, as well as the desiccator that had contained the cyanide. Roget merely stepped over the ruined equipment and the broken glass, carrying his case of frogs back towards the passage door.

He did not appear to have control of his movements.

Leaving a trail of destruction behind him, Roget balanced the glass case awkwardly over one hip as he opened the door and stepped out into the corridor.

Here he paused again, his head cocked on one side, as if listening for instructions.

Roget straightened, carrying the case in both hands now, and walked back down the corridor, footsteps echoing. He came out into the lobby and without hesitating turned left and went straight to the door that bore the sign "Matron." He went in, pausing only to kick the door closed behind him.

Doctor Roget set the glass case down on Matron Cassidy's oak desk, sweeping piles of papers and files to the floor to make a clear space. He unclamped the lid, waited, looking up towards the ceiling where the fluorescent tube was flickering, then reached out slowly with his right hand and picked up the jade dragon paperweight.

With his left hand, Roget took out one of the frogs, gripping it tightly. The animal croaked and then gave a high, keening sound of pure fear.

He held its rear legs and crushed the jade paperweight down onto its head, splashing blood and gristle across the desk and onto the front of his white coat. He kept pounding, and pounding, his face dull, trance-like . . .

The lift dropped twice as far as last time and the jar as it jerked to a stop slammed through Ed's tortured body, bringing a croak of pain to his split lips.

Jesus, thought Ed woozily, I wish it would fall all the way and get it over with!

But the image of the crunching impact made him shudder and the motion brought him sitting upright. In turn, the pain of the sudden movement knifed into his consciousness and he focused his eyes on his mangled hands, blinking as the light in the ceiling flickered wildly.

The burning numbness was spreading up from his forearms into his biceps and shoulders now. He reckoned it must be the carbon monoxide taking over as his body used up more and more oxygen from his bloodstream. Hell, there couldn't be much left now.

But, for a raging moment, he was damned if he was

160

going to give up! He had always been a battler, had fought every bit of the way for what little he had.

Now he had to fight for his life.

He leaned sideways, brushing aside the dead and withered flowers, fingers clawing, straining to reach the grip rail he had ripped out of the wall. He touched it but the thick bandages would not allow him to grab it, the cloth made his fingers slip off the metal. He did not have enough strength to crawl over there.

Gasping, feeling drugged, Ed tore at the bandages with his teeth, gagging on the taste, but freeing the cloth strips. Then he tried again and managed to hook his fingers into the bend of the bar where it had been fixed to the wall. It clanged dully as he dragged it towards him.

It seemed hours before he had enough strength to hitch himself around on his buttocks. Then, he didn't know how much later, he managed to bring the rail around and he inserted the heavy lug end of the bracket into the crack at the bottom of the doors and threw his weight across it.

He was surprised when the door moved a fraction, just a few millimetres, but for their full length. A cold draught hissed in, a bare trickle, but more air than there had been.

As he fell forward, his face against the cold metal, windpipe seared by the meagre air flow, the lift lurched violently and started to plunge down the shaft.

In Room 15 the EEG pens scribbled wildly across the graph paper. Needles on the dials flicked and jerked. The heart-activity monitor peaked and beeped with light waves.

Sweat soaked Patrick's body, trickled down his face. The sheet was sodden where it draped over him. His eyes seemed to have a fierce concentration as if he was fighting to hold onto something—perhaps more than he could control.

It was as if he was dividing his attention, spreading his power in several directions and finding it difficult to maintain everything.

161

There was a heavy *clank-thump!* from somewhere outside the room and then the needles on the dials steadied at about the half-way mark. The heart monitor lines eased back to a series of steady beats and the graph needles registered strong and regular activity.

The intense look seemed to ease from Patrick's face. Whatever conflict had taken place, he appeared to have emerged in full control again.

Kathy slammed the Chrysler to a stop outside the closed gates of the clinic, driving the car's off-side wheels up onto the kerb. She did not bother locking the door as she got out and ran to the gates, fumbling at the catch.

As she ran up the path, she glanced towards the window above the unlit EMERGENCY sign. She tensed as she saw the end of the stainless steel drip-bottle stand jutting out of the window. Hoping she was not too late, Kathy burst into the lobby and stopped to lean on the reception desk, trying to steady her breathing, looking around.

She saw the wires dangling from the switchboard. The whole place had a deserted look and feel to it. There was a sort of dull clank from the lift shaft. She instinctively looked at the quivering wall indicator. It appeared to be jammed between the first and ground floors. The "Out of Order" sign seemed to glare at her.

Kathy headed for the stairs but stopped as she heard a noise coming from Matron Cassidy's office. It was a rhythmic thumping sound. Tense and trembling, she turned towards the door, gripped the knob with both hands and twisted it. She hesitated a moment, then thrust the door open violently and went inside.

Roget was at Matron's desk, his back to her. He seemed to be smashing at something in front of him.

"Doctor?" she called tentatively.

The pounding stopped and she moved warily across the office, stepping to one side so she could see what he was doing. Kathy felt her stomach heave involuntarily and her face screwed up as she saw the gory mess on top of the desk. Then, his eyes dull, Roget lifted his face and she saw the blood around his mouth, on his chin and down the front of his white coat. Even as she looked, he picked up a shattered, raw frog and lifted it mechanically towards his mouth.

Kathy leapt forward and slapped it from his hand, at the same time smashing him across the face. "Stop it!" she gagged. "In the name of God! What are you *doing?*"

She was disgusted, sickened and repelled.

Roget blinked at her and put a shaking hand to his face where she had struck him. Suddenly, the dullness seemed to go from his eyes and he looked down in horror at the slaughter on the desk, his hands dripping with blood and pieces of flesh. He grimaced and wiped them on his white coat.

"It was *him!*" he whispered. *"He* made me do it!"

Kathy stepped backwards as he moved towards her, his voice pleading for her understanding.

"Don't you see? It was *Patrick!* He has taken control . . ."

Kathy stared and then abruptly shook herself out of the horrified mood. "Taken control?" she echoed, and immediately ran for the door.

Roget leapt after her. "Don't go near him! He will kill you!"

But Kathy ran on out of the office and Roget went after her, calling as she headed for the stairs and went up them two at a time. Kathy's breath sobbed in her throat as she climbed, using the rails to help her. She still carried the picture of Roget's blood-flecked face, and wondered just what fate Patrick had for her husband . . .

She reached the second floor, panting, and stumbled a little before hurrying down the passage. Behind her, Roget staggered up the stairs.

"We have got to kill him!" he shouted, his voice echoing hollowly. "We will get the patients out, set fire to the building! You have to help me!"

He clung to the rail at the top of the stairs, fighting for breath, swaying, his eyes bulging as Kathy went straight to the door of Room 15.

"It is no use!" Roget called hoarsely. "He has sealed himself in."

Kathy jiggled the door knob violently.

The door opened inwards.

Roget's mouth sagged open. "It is a trap!" he screamed.

Kathy stepped aside.

The door slammed closed like a bank vault sealing itself with an automatic and impregnable mechanism.

Chapter Seventeen

Kathy stopped just inside Room 15, staring at the shattered pot and the crushed plant, the glittering handle of the hypodermic syringe showing under the bed, the broken drip bottles and the bent stand jutting out of the window above the EMERGENCY sign, the chair lying on its side.

She stared, too, at the graph paper rolling out of the EEG unit, seeing the peaks and valleys of Patrick's brain activity. The other monitor dials showed much more powerful readings than she had seen since coming to the clinic. She wrenched her gaze away and set her cold eyes on Patrick who was still wearing his EEG head harness. A dial registered an extremely rapid pulse rate.

"What have you done to my husband?" she gritted.

There was a thumping on the door and she knew Roget was vainly trying to get in. Patrick had somehow locked it, but that suited Kathy. She wanted to be alone with him now. She walked to the side of the bed, looked down at him, suddenly very calm.

"I want an answer, Patrick."

Then she went to the typewriter, plugged it in, switched it on and rolled a sheet of paper into the carriage.

"Where is he?" she asked angrily.

The she swiftly lifted her arms across her face as a whole ream of typing paper was rapidly blown in her direction, a page at a time, with the speed of a berserk machine-gun. She slapped the last few sheets irritably aside from her face, grabbed the ends of the typewriter carriage in an effort to prevent him ejecting the paper she had rolled in.

"Talk to me, Patrick, damn you! *Talk to me!*"

She jumped as the typewriter rattled and the ball leapt in a burst of speed, printing out:

GET FUCKED, YOU SLUT!

Kathy whirled to face him. "Is that what you think I am? A slut?"

Patrick made a single, emphatic spitting sound.

"Why, for God's sake?" she asked, genuinely puzzled. "Because I was with another man? Because I don't belong to you?" Then it was like a revelation and she moved over close to him. When she spoke her voice was icy, sure. "That is why you murdered your own mother, isn't it, Patrick? Because she went with other men, wasn't exclusively yours, was a slut!"

Kathy gasped as all the cupboard doors flew open and glassware and papers and instruments shrieked across the room in the savage storm of Patrick's anger. The whole room seemed to vibrate and she grabbed at the desk for support. There was a deep rumbling that racked right through her body, from somewhere beneath her feet, jerking her head on her shoulders. Plaster flaked off the walls and ceiling in a miniature snow storm.

The violence did not seem to be aimed at Kathy; it was almost as if it wasn't meant to injure her, but to impress her. She was frightened but determined and refused to show that this demonstration had awed her in any way. She took a deep breath.

"Now we are getting somewhere!"

She noticed that the peaks and valleys on the rolling graph paper as it piled up in the receiving trays were slightly smaller. Patrick had apparently expended considerable energy on his demonstration.

She thought she heard the lift motor clank briefly.

The pulse rate had dropped too and the other monitors showed erratic readings. Kathy felt a stir of triumph in her. There *was* a way to fight Patrick, it

166

seemed. *If* he could be coaxed into expending the energy he had ben building up all these years . . .

"What do you think, Patrick?" she asked quietly, her voice still edged with frost. "That if you stopped other men from getting to me then we would be together for ever and ever?"

The monitor dials flickered wildly. The needles on the graph paper jerked from one side of the page to the other.

Kathy picked up the withered cyclamen, held it out. "I realize now how this plant could bloom one minute and be dead the next. You were using it as a kind of barometer, weren't you? Of my behaviour. When I was 'good' in your book, the flower bloomed. When I did something you did not approve of, you killed it . . . The same as you wrecked my flat, tried to drown Brian Wright, and burned Ed's hands." Her voice rose despite herself. *"Where is he?"*

The typewriter rattled and Kathy ran to it, noticing with an edge of her mind that Roget had stopped hammering on the door. The typewriter had printed:

I LOVE YOU.

Kathy turned slowly, was silent for a long moment. Then she folded her arms and leaned back against the desk edge. "Love? What do you know about love? And who could love *you*? Your own mother couldn't stand you! You are arrogant and vindictive! You, you are self-centred, self-indulgent and self-important!"

Kathy's eyes flicked to the gauges and dials of the monitors. They wavered without synchronization and she saw his blood-pressure reading begin to rise.

"Just who the hell do you think you are, anyway? If you are so bloody clever, stand up like a man and tell me *who the hell you are?*"

The needles jumped several times. Patrick made a rapid series of angry spitting sounds.

"You are Doctor Roget's electric train set, Patrick, that is all you are!" Kathy told him sardonically, provoking him. "Some doctors play golf, some have vintage cars, or speed-boats, but Doctor Roget has Patrick to play with! And now he wants to discard you

167

like a toy he has grown tired of! And who the hell could blame him?"

The chair whipped across the room, narrowly missing Kathy and shattering the glass doors of the cabinet above the desk. She jumped aside as glass rained down. Containers and reagent bottles from the bench near the sink smashed against the wall in a rapid-fire series of dull explosions. Kathy cringed until the last one fell to the floor. Her hair was dishevelled now and she was breathing fast.

The monitor and dials registered insane activity.

The lift motor clanked several times.

"Go on!" she breathed. "Get it out of your system! Your tantrums no longer scare me, Patrick!"

There was a sudden silence in the room and Kathy approached the bed again, determined. "What have you done to Ed?"

The typewriter rattled.

BOXED-IN, HUNG-UP. HA-HA!

She clenched her fists, wondering if she could sustain her anger. She was badly frightened and wondered if he could sense her true feelings. *"Where is he?"*

The typewriter printed:

DO YOU LOVE HIM?

"Yes!" Kathy said without hesitation.

The typewriter clattered:

WOULD YOU DIE TO SAVE HIM?

Kathy felt her jaw sag a little, shocked by the question. Frowning, she nodded, swallowed and said in a quiet, but emphatic voice, "Yes I would."

GOOD printed the typewriter.

Kathy frowned, subconsciously noticing that the brain activity was registering less than it had been. The needles seemed to give sudden, erratic jerks, as if there was a massive strain on Patrick's powers now as he tried to control so many things at the same time.

"What, what does that mean?" Kathy asked.

UNDER THE BED, printed the typewriter and Kathy, frowning, saw the hypodermic syringe amongst the broken glass and earth from the flower pot. She

168

stooped and picked it up, feeling suddenly strange, a little out-of-step with reality. She fought the feeling.

"You mean this? What is it?"

CYANIDE SOLUTION. QUICK. PAINLESS.

"Patrick, I don't understand!"

SIMPLE. TIME IS RUNNING OUT. ED OR PATRICK. DECIDE.

Kathy, still holding the needle, fighting off the lethargy that was creeping through her body, looked at him in sad bewilderment.

"Patrick, I couldn't kill you!"

The typewriter clattered very fast, in a prolonged burst.

YET EACH MAN KILLS THE THING HE LOVES
BY EACH LET THIS BE HEARD
SOME DO IT WITH A BITTER LOOK
SOME WITH A FLATTERING WORD
THE COWARD DOES IT WITH A KISS
THE BRAVE MAN WITH A SWORD

Kathy stared at the words, vaguely registering that it was from the works of Oscar Wilde, but she obviously did not understand what Patrick expected of her. She put a hand to her head.

"Let me think, Patrick!" she stalled. "Tell me about Ed . . ."

DECIDE printed the machine, underlining the word.

Kathy sagged back against the desk, the syringe held loosely down at her side in one hand, the other rubbing at her forehead.

"Wait," she said, surprised at how weak her own voice sounded, aware that something was trying to take control. Patrick, of course. But she was fighting as hard as she could.

The needles on the graph paper were making more regular sweeps now, the lines wavy, rather than angular. The heart monitor screen showed lower activity, the pulse rate was straining to keep a high level.

Sweat drenched Patrick as he fought to maintain control.

Then Kathy's eyes turned downwards to look at the

syringe. Her hand seemed to want to rise of its own accord.

Detective Sergeant Grant's car screeched wildly around the corner into the side street. He straightened the wheels and gunned the motor down to the clinic, seeing the orange Chrysler half on the foopath.

His face was grim. He had been held up in the office after Kathy's last phone call and by the time he got away peak-hour traffic was moving at snail's pace and he reckoned he must have sweated off three kilograms getting here. As he kicked open the door and leapt out, he noticed that it was almost dusk but there seemed to be only a few lights on in the clinic. Grant ran up the path and went in through the open front doors, seeing the deserted lobby and the "Out of Order" sign on the lift doors.

He ran for the stairs and, as he neared the bottom of them, stopped. There was a clank and a whir from the lift shaft. He looked at the indicator. The lift was coming down. Grant veered over there, pushed the button automatically and stepped back to await its arrival.

The steel doors began to open automatically and Grant swore in surprise as Ed Jacquard fell out backwards and landed at his feet, half in and half out of the lift. His face had a bluish tinge and there was a rasping, mucous gurgling coming from his throat. As Grant knelt beside him, he began to cough violently, his face congested and his eyes started from his head, as, for the first time in two days, fresh air entered his lungs. After so many sudden drops, he could not believe the lift had brought him down safely. He felt like weeping.

"What the hell happened to you?" Grant snapped. Then, realization suddenly hit him. "You're Ed Jacquard?"

Managing to control his coughing a little, clawing at his seared throat, Ed nodded slowly.

"Shit!" Grant breathed, feeling an unaccountable cold shiver run down his spine.

Kathy started as the typewriter suddenly made a brief, staccato sound. The needle was half-raised towards her bent left arm and she let it drop down to her side again, turning to see what the typewriter had printed out this time.

THE COWARD DOES IT WITH A KISS

She still felt strange, trance-like, although she fought hard. She felt that some of the force trying to control her was weakening and turned her head slowly to look at the monitors. Pulse rate was dropping, the heart monitor showed low activity, blood pressure was down, the EEG needles were weakly erratic.

The typewriter clattered again, but it was slower, more deliberate, like a two-finger expert, taking time to search for each key. The message was brief.

I'M GOING NOW.

I LOVE YOU.

COME WITH ME.

Helplessly, Kathy began to lift the hypodermic needle, feeling a little faint. She was vaguely aware of voices outside in the passage but could not make out any words.

It was Grant and Roget. The detective, once he made sure Ed was going to be all right, had come upstairs alone, leaving Ed to recover in the lobby. Grant was shocked to see Roget sitting down in the passage opposite the door of Room 15, blood-spattered, looking wild, insane.

"What the bloody hell happened to you?"

Roget looked at him silently, and then semed to focus his eyes on Grant properly and stir himself out of his daze. He held up a hand and the policeman heaved him to his feet. Roget steadied himself against the wall.

"You all right?" Grant asked.

Roget nodded unsteadily.

"Mrs. Jacquard?"

171

Roget gestured towards the door of Room 15. "He has got her in there. Trapped."

"Who?" Grant snapped.

"Patrick!" Roget shouted wildly. "He will kill her!" He was breathing raggedly now. "Matron was right to try and kill him! He is evil! He will control us all if . . ."

Grant slapped him hard across the face and Roget reeled back, blinking. But the shock snapped him out of it and his eyes took a more sane look as he straightened his coat. He turned to the door and tried the handle. It would not move.

"We can't get in," he said quietly. "He has locked the door somehow. Even the master key won't work."

Grant pushed Roget aside, hammered on the door with his fist. "Mrs. Jacquard? You in there? You all right?"

"Wait!" Roget said suddenly, running to the end of the corridor and going around the corner. Here there was a fire axe in a glass case on the wall and he wrapped a handkerchief around his knuckles and smashed his hand through the glass. He took out the axe and ran back down the corridor, almost knocking over old Captain Fraser as the man shuffled out of his door in his greatcoat and slouch hat, tap-dragging his walking aid.

"Give it to 'em, boys!" The Captain shouted after Roget's running figure. "Drive back the Hun! Hold 'em at bay! No retreat now!"

Grant frowned at the old man and started to speak, but Roget pushed him aside and attacked the door with the axe. The blade bounced off the wood as if were steel. It did not leave a mark.

"What the hell . . . !" exclaimed Grant, incredulous, not believing his eyes as Roget swung the axe time after time and the blade merely bounced off the wood. Still there were no marks. He looked a little grey as he glanced at Roget. "What, what is going on in this bloody madhouse?"

Roget, panting, leaning weakly on the axe handle, shaking his head slowly, unable to speak.

Then Grant looked past him as Ed Jacquard's dishevelled and wild-looking figure came staggering down the corridor from the direction of the stairs.

Ed propped himself against the wall and stared as Roget suddenly lifted the axe and delivered one massive final blow at the door. The blade turned, skidded off and Roget fell against the wall, dropping the axe. Puzzled, Ed looked at Grant.

"What's going on?" he croaked.

"Your wife is in there," Grant said grimly. "We can't get the door open."

"Kathy?" Ed seemed to come to life, jostled between Roget and Grant and went to the door. He grabbed the handle and shook it. *"Kathy!"* he shouted.

The door opened. Roget and Grant stared open-mouthed as Ed lurched into Room 15. They leapt after him.

Kathy, with a dazed look on her face was lowering the needle of the hypodermic towards the big vein in the crook of her left arm. Roget recognized the syringe instantly and, with a cry, lunged across the room, falling to his knees, reaching out desperately and knocking the instrument from her grasp. It smashed on the floor and there was the pungent odour of bitter almonds.

Kathy started at the sudden movement, spun to face the men and blinked as she recognized Ed. Her lips parted and her knees buckled. Ed grabbed her. Grant caught her other side and between them they supported her. Then she looked at her husband, threw her arms weakly around his neck and buried her face against his chest, sobbing.

Roget stood very close to the bed, leaning over Patrick.

The graph paper had stopped moving, the heart lines on the monitor screen were simply lines, the needles on the dials were all at zero.

"He's gone," Roget said and there was vast relief in his tone as he straightened and looked at Grant. "Dead at last!"

"That was Patrick?" Grant asked, and at Roget's

nod, added, "Well, I don't understand any of this, Doctor. There are a lot of questions I want answered."

Kathy's sobs quietened and she searched for a hand-kerchief to wipe her eyes. Ed held her awkwardly with his sore hands.

"It's simple enough, Sergeant," Roget said. "A patient has died, that is all."

"Bull, that is all!" Grant snapped. "That 'patient' as you call him is listed on our books as a homicidal maniac! And look at this room: it looks like someone drove a truck through it! And what about that hypo full of cyanide? Coming on top of Matron Cassidy's queer death and that nurse in a state of hysteria, I reckon it is anything *but* simple!"

Roget looked at Kathy who was dabbing her eyes. Ed stared around, looking only briefly at the pale, wax-like Patrick who was still wearing the EEG head harness and wires. Ed let his eyes follow the tubes and electrodes emerging from the giant cannula still fixed to Patrick's neck. They led his gaze to the bent steel drip-bottle stand, the wires wrapped around its shaft, as it protruded out of the window into the dusk.

He did not understand any of it. But he didn't care. All he cared about was the fact that Kathy was safe, in his arms . . . Roget and Grant began to argue quietly. . . .

Downstairs, old Captain Fraser shuffled up to the side entrance door of the clinic, gripped the polished brass knob in his shaky hand and opened it. He moved his walking-aid forward onto the porch and stepped out, staring around at the darkening sky, shot through with writhing colours of afterglow.

Yes, it was time for him to do his nightly duty and switch on the EMERGENCY sign. He hadn't missed doing it in nigh on twenty years and he wasn't going to let The Hun stop him now, even though the attack seemed to be in real earnest, judging by all that noise and violence he had heard in Room 15 before he came down. Serve that bloke right if he got killed any-way, bloody spy for The Hun, that's all he was . . .

Captain Fraser opened the meter box and balanced

himself against his walking aid as he reached up, grabbed the sign's switch and pulled it down firmly with deep satisfaction.

Above his head, there was a fizzle and crackle as the neon gas in the tubing writhed and lit up, but suddenly there was a violet-blue flash, a shower of sparks and the shattering of glass.

The end of the stainless steel drip-bottle stand, jutting out of the window of Room 15, had broken part of the neon tubing at the terminal end. As the electricity surged through the sign, it shorted out in a violent thunderbolt that streaked along the stainless steel stand, and through the wires and tubes still connected to the cannula and electrodes in Patrick's neck.

Kathy screamed as Patrick jerked bolt upright in the bed, eyes staring from his head, lips peeled back, teeth bared in a maniacal grin. His arms flung into the air, sending the sheet flying, and his whole body hurtled off the bed straight at the group of rigid people. Claw-like fingers sought a throat to squeeze as the four people fell over each other in an effort to get away from the insane thing that pursued them . . .

Then Patrick fell limply to the floor.

Hearts pounding, they stood there shakily, looking down at Patrick's inert form.

"What the bloody hell was *that?*" creaked Ed, shaking almost as much as Kathy as she clung tightly to him.

Roget touched Patrick's flesh with the back of his hand, the way electricians test a piece of machinery to make sure it isn't electrified. He glanced up at Grant and the others.

"Just a muscular response," he said quietly. "I have seen it before."

He glanced at Kathy and, though the turmoil in her head, she had a picture of a dead frog leaping at her, in this very room, when Roget applied an electric stimulus to it.

Roget motioned to Grant to lend a hand and they lifted Patrick back onto the bed. The doctor looked down at him.

"Some people might say it was the life force, or the soul departing the body . . . I don't know. Anyway, it's over now."

Grant sighed heavily. "Look, Doctor, you just sign the Death Certificate and get that . . . thing . . . buried as soon as possible, okay?" He wiped his face with a shaking hand.

Roget nodded, glanced once more at Patrick, and motioned for Grant to come with him. They left and Ed urged Kathy towards the door. She pulled out of his grip and went to the bed and smoothed Patrick's hair back off his forehead. It was still marked from the EEG harness.

She closed his eyelids gently, stood for a moment beside the bed, then turned and followed the others out into the passage, leaving the door open. She took Ed's arm and held it tightly as they walked towards the stairs.

In Room 15, amidst the wreckage scattered around the floor, Patrick lay at peace on the bed, flat on his back, eyes closed, a breeze from the smashed window gently stirring his hair.

Then, slowly, his eyes opened and stared fixedly up at the ceiling.

A moment later, the door to Room 15 closed silently of its own accord.